Hybrid

First Rare Wolf

K J Carr

Cover Art by SelfPubBookCovers.com/ van_maniac

Prologue

Shane

"Move! Move! Move!"

Baron's augmented Alpha powers hit me at the same time the roar came over my communicator, giving me a headache. I hated when he augmented his powers. I was on the fucking other side of the building! I just hoped he wasn't coming up fast behind me, because I needed time.

I snorted. No fucking way I was going to stop now. Not until I found what I had come here to retrieve. I would challenge him for Alpha before I would stop searching and God knows, I didn't want his job.

I kept moving further down the hallway, opening

doors frantically, checking inside quickly, and then moving onto the next door. They had to be here!

"Shane! Boomer has set the timers! We are out of time!"

This time, the power in the command caused me to stagger, almost turning back. I growled, righting myself. I ignored my Alpha's command. Not going to leave without them. I tried using my nose, but human noses aren't as sensitive as wolf ones. Besides, the ammonia smell tickled my nose. One good sniff and I would be sneezing. After the first five times this had happened, I decided that shallow breaths were better.

This lab, which performed illegal experiments, shouldn't exist, and yet it did. It wasn't on any government or private list, anywhere. The lab was a ghost. It would pop up and then shut down at a moment's notice. If it wasn't for Shaz, we wouldn't have found it this time.

Someone had discovered that lycanthropes existed. That same someone had targeted us for inhumane experimentation. They captured, or in this case, murdered, wolves in order to get their test subjects.

When they fucked with my family, though, I was

going to move heaven and hell to get them back.

"Shane!"

The shout turned almost into a howl, the Alpha's power causing me to stagger again. Damn it! He was closing in behind me. I sped up my search, my heart pounding.

My insubordination was going to bring me a world of hurt later, but I didn't care. Being Beta suited me. I didn't want to be Alpha. Even if we both knew that I would win.

I just didn't want it. Way too much responsibility of people I cared little about. But I wasn't stopping my search yet.

A slim grey wolf slid up next to me, its long and lanky form hiding slightly in the shadows. Shaz. He yipped softly at me, his eyes glinting, his tongue rolling out of his mouth. I growled at him, not stopping. He put his body in front of mine, forcing me to either run him over or stop. I stopped, my growl growing louder. He rolled his eyes and then darted forward down the hall.

I watched him as he passed several doors before pausing and looking over his shoulder at me. Looked like he knew where he was going. I followed, my two feet not as fast as his four. As soon as he saw this, he continued loping down the hallway.

Shaz stopped in front of a reinforced metal door, almost at the end. He sat, panting, his eyes gleaming as if to say 'This is it'.

My hand went to the door handle, but it didn't budge. Locked. Damn it! I pounded on it once in frustration.

Lock picks. Where did I put them? I started patting my pockets, searching for them.

The wolf shook his head, snorting in derision. He quickly shifted, the naked man crouching in the dim and dusty light.

He stood, not caring about his lack of clothes, and grabbed a key that hung to the left of the door and shoved it in front of my face.

"Oh, Oblivious One."

I stared at the key. My eyes traveled to the spot where it had been hanging and then back to the man grinning wildly in front of me.

"Seriously? They left the key here? Just outside the door?"

Shaz shrugged. “They are stupid assholes, Shane. What did you expect?”

I snorted, snatching the key out of his hand. It took me a minute to push it in, with my hand trembling with exhaustion, but it finally clicked in the lock. I pushed the door open slowly.

The darkness in the room overpowered my human sight, but the smells of urine and excrement permeating the air were noticeable even in this form. I walked in warily, my eyes flicking from shadow to shadow, my hands slightly outstretched. Right now, I really wished I had my wolf’s ability to see in the dark.

Shaz stumbled behind me, swearing loudly as he searched for a light switch. The thought of what was on these floors caused me to cringe.

Fucking hell!” The man growled. The sound of a desk being shoved violently came from behind me. Items rolled to the floor and then a click sounded.

A narrow beam of light illuminated the room.

Great. Shaz had found a flashlight. Definitely useful here.

In the next minute, he clicked on a light switch

and the weak light from overhead lit the room. I almost wished for the darkness, given what I was seeing.

Syringes and vials laid over on one counter. A table that still had remnants of blood and gore stood in the middle. A computer sat at another station in a far corner, its screen blank.

"Over there." I moved towards one wall, where I saw large cages stacked together. The doors on the top two swung open, empty.

"Hurry up, Shane. Boomer never gives us much time once he's set his bombs. We need to be out of here yesterday." Shaz's eyes roamed nervously around the room.

I move closer to the cages. It was not an option to leave. Not at this point. "Can you use that flashlight and shine it down here?" I knelt and opened the bottom cage's door.

Shaz shuffled closer, pointing his flashlight where I wanted it. I sat down cross-legged in front of the cage.

Three small pups laid on a dirty blanket, motionless. Their ribs showed through the scraggly patches of their fur. They looked.... Dead.

No! It couldn't be too late!

I held my breath, my hand lying gently on the nearest pup's chest, counting out the seconds. One... Two.... Three....

There! A shuttering, croaky breath came from that one. Then another pup exhaled softly.

No time to check on the third. I reached in, pulling out the small male pup first.

"Take Soren, Shaz. I will get the two girls."

"Oh, man!" He looked down at the small pup in his hands, his eyes wide with shock.

My eyes glinted with anger as I gazed at the pup. "I really hate these self-entitled fuckers. But to use pups!" I shook my head, trying to get my emotions back under control.

I reached in and picked up the larger of the two females. Betta. She appeared to be in a similar condition as her brother. I checked her over quickly before laying her gently on one thigh.

It was the last pup, though, where my heart almost broke. Lexi was so dehydrated and starved, she looked like a skeleton. I couldn't tell if she was even still alive. I was afraid to touch her; she looked so fragile.

No matter. She was coming with me, dead or alive.

Leave no one behind.

The room's door slammed open, hitting the wall behind it. Shaz took a protective stance while holding Soren. I curled over Betta, who was in my lap, while leaning towards the cage where Lexi still laid.

A large, stocky man stormed in. He snarled softly. "When I told you to leave, I meant now. Those bombs will explode in sixty seconds, whether we have left the building. We need to be in Timbuktu, you fucking asshats!"

Both of us relaxed, Shaz moving carefully towards his Alpha.

"Grab a pup from Shane, Baron. We will move faster if we each have one. But, be careful. They are in terrible shape." He exited the room, his voice wafting back as he moved down the hallway. "There's an exit down here that we can use, I think."

Baron turned to me, moving closer. He gasped as I handed Betta up to him, holding her tiny body with two huge hands.

"Take Betta, Baron. I need to get Lexi out of there, but I am afraid I will hurt her when I pick her up."

Baron's eyes filled with sorrow as he clasped the small female to his chest, moving to the door. "We won't do them any good if we all get blown up inside this building. I don't want to leave it standing. Gather up your pup, Shane, and let's move."

I moved to kneel beside the cage and gently reached in to lift out Lexi. The small female was so light, I was afraid I would hurt her without trying. Standing, I pulled my T-shirt up to wrap it around her, making a pouch out of it to protect her small body. I followed behind the other two men, my strides long.

"Thirty seconds!"

Shaz stood near an outside door, the sunlight streaming in. I blinked. I felt like I had spent a lifetime in this house of horrors. The bright sunny day outside seemed wrong in contrast.

Baron and I jogged towards the door, exiting before Shaz closed it carefully.

"That's a firewall door. Hopefully, it will help keep the debris away when the building blows but run like hell, boys, because we have little time."

We scrambled for the tree line about fifty yards away. It was a trade-off; either run fast and jostle the pups or run slower and have the explosion blow us to pieces.

We ran like the devil was on our tails. No saving the pups if we died in the explosion.

We had barely passed the first few trees when the first bomb went off, rocking the ground.

I fell, twisting in the air so I would land on my back, protecting Lexi as much as I could. Shaz barely kept his feet, pausing when he saw I had gone down.

"Off your back, Shane. No time to be lazing around. Second blow is going to happen in about ten."

Baron had already disappeared into the woods.

"Move it!" The Alpha bellowed, his voice easily reaching us.

A white and black wolf darted out of the woods, heading for me. He shifted as he got within a few steps of me. Reaching down, the man helped me stand, peering at the bundle being held close to my chest.

"Fuck!"

"Splinter, Shane, now!" Baron's voice was further off, but still held authority.

Without thought, we turned and ran into the woods, heading towards the Alpha. A second explosion sounded behind us, followed closely by a third.

We barely kept to our feet, dodging rocks and debris that came raining down on us. Splinter reached out to keep me steady, matching my steps. We reached a gravel road and quickly moved towards a lone SUV.

"Left that a little close, didn't you?" The man leaning up against the driver-side door grinned at us. "You know my babies like to make a splash."

"Let's get out of here, Boomer!" Baron snarled, taking shotgun and carefully laying Betta gently on his lap.

Boomer leapt into the car and started it, his face turning serious as he took in Betta's condition.

"Shit."

Shaz and I slid into the back, holding our bundles carefully. I kept Lexi wrapped in my shirt, figuring the more structure she had, the better. Splinter squeezed into the back, leaning over the seat to look at the pups, his face serious.

"Where is Max?" I couldn't help it. The words came out as a growl.

As soon as the doors shut, the car took off, the wheels churning in the gravel on the road. Boomer hit the phone button on the steering wheel.

"Call Max."

I thanked the gods we had the satellite phones. The call went through immediately. "Hey, Max? Where are you located? Shane found the pups. They are half-dead."

Another explosion rocked the truck.

"Shit! That wasn't one of mine. They probably had a gas of some sort in that lab." Boomer struggled to keep the car upright and on the road, speeding up again once the ground had stopped rocking. The phone crackled and popped with static, causing us to miss what was being said.

"... meeting point."

"Max, this is Boomer. Sorry, we had another, unplanned explosion here. You're at the meeting point? Good. Plan to get into our truck with your bag of goodies. We have three pups..." He looked over at Baron, sitting next to him, gently stroking Betta's ragged fur. He swallowed. "... Three pups that are looking terrible. I am not sure if you can even save them. Sorry, Shane."

He threw the last remark over his shoulder at me.

I ignored him, watching Lexi's chest. I wanted to breathe for her, but I couldn't. I checked to make sure she was doing it on her own, placing two fingers on her tiny chest. One... two.... three.... four.... five... I felt a slight movement beneath my fingers, causing me to inhale as well.

How was she still alive? I rubbed her chest to stimulate her body a little.

"Come on, Lexi. Uncle Shane is here. I've got you. I've got all of you. Please live. You are all strong pups. You must live."

I didn't realize I was mumbling this to her, my voice soft and insistent as I pulled her close to my body heat. I refused to think about my brother and his wife - the pup's parents - who were murdered, probably right in front of these pups. My brother had wanted to start a Pack and had left to build his own den. Someone had killed them in that den and left to rot, their pups taken and experimented on.

Revenge for what they had done to my family burned in my chest.

I pulled Lexi closer. "You're safe now, little one. Uncle Shane has your back."

Chapter 1

Holden

I looked out the French doors at the three small pups. My heart, which had shattered not that long ago, broke again, seeing them. Someone had created a den for them on the deck, near enough that we could easily see them from where we were in the house.

"They have gone through a tough time."

The tall man on my right stood with his hands shoved in his pockets. He was watching the three wolf pups sleeping on a blanket in the sun outside of their den. Their little legs would twitch every so often, but not as if they were running or playing in their dreams. No, it was more like they were having a seizure or were trying to remove their legs from someone's hands. A few whimpers floated up before they would move closer together and fall back into a deeper sleep.

I stood beside him, studying the pups. I could count every rib on all three of them. Even from where I stood, at least five feet away. I didn't know why they were in this condition yet. The men had just said it was confidential and they would tell me once I had arrived here, if I would come. So, here I am.

These pups were worse off than my employers had revealed, and what they had said had told me they had been in an unpleasant situation.

I would do whatever I could to make these little ones well again.

A large bowl of water sat next to them, along with a bowl of small meat cubes. Both bowls were still full, though. I had watched the doctor, who was standing on my left, put the bowls out when I had first arrived only ten minutes ago, but the pups hadn't awakened.

The smallest pup seemed to stop breathing every so often, the pause long before she took another shuttering breath. I breathed with her, counting out the seconds of that pause, urging the little pup to take a breath each time. I gasped.

The doctor, Max, shook his head, touching my arm gently before dropping his hand.

"Don't watch Lexi breathe. She has a respiratory issue going on that I haven't yet figured out. Everyone who watches her end up breathing in sync with her, trying to get her to take that next breath whenever she stops breathing. It only makes us hyperventilate."

Lexi. I wondered exactly what Lexi and her siblings had been through when the man on my other side continued.

"We rescued them from an experimental laboratory that had taken them after killing their parents. All three were in a cage too small for even one of them. Researchers poked, prodded and cruelly tested drugs on them." His voice was like a low growl.

I glanced up at him, my eyes flitting from his silver hair to his silver eyes to those sensuous lips. He pressed those lips into a firm line. He had an unique attractiveness. His strange hair and eye color were mesmerizing. I felt myself leaning towards him. Wanting to study him in more detail.

No, it was too soon. I pulled my clinical persona over my broken soul to study the man beside me.

This was a man who had experienced things that had marked his soul. His face looked too young for him to have silver hair, and yet he did. I wondered if it was natural or if it resulted from trauma. I knew that trauma did strange things to people.

I felt more than heard the soft whine in my head. Not now. I had been hearing wolves in my head since my husband had died. I wasn't sure why. I pushed the thought away, ignoring it. *Don't go crazy now, Holden*.

Sighing, I turned back to watch the pups. Even with his strange eyes and hair, something was familiar about his face. I just wasn't sure what it was. I wasn't sure if I wanted to know. Not now. But I was sure I had met him before, at least for a fleeting moment. The thought tickled my mind before I pushed that away. Now was the time to learn about the pups, not me. Not my problems.

He didn't seem to notice that I had been watching him since he continued talking.

"Max examined them after we had gotten them out. Those idiots had taken a lot of blood and had injected the pups with various toxins, as their blood tests shown. It had taken us a few weeks before we were even sure they would survive. There may be long-term issues that we can only speculate about. Only time will tell."

His intense anger filled the room with the emotion and strangled me. This was another one of those things that had changed recently. Feeling the emotions of others. I could feel his anger beating against my skin and almost taste it on my tongue. I had felt an emotion like this before, but nothing like this. My husband had been easygoing, except his anger had been this quiet burn, slowly growing. At some point, it would come out, filling up a room and smothering me with its intensity. I wasn't sure if I was just empathic or if everyone could feel emotion like this. At least a little. I couldn't tell if I was feeling the pups or this man right now. It was such a mixture of anger, sadness, sorrow, and hurt.

"Shane." Max chastised, his voice controlled and low. Shane exhaled, releasing the tension that had been filling the room. Interesting. I glanced at Max, wondering if he had also felt the emotion.

If there was someone else like me. Well, he was a doctor. I suspected he knew a little about mental illness.

I inhaled deeply. I would not ask him about it, though. In fact, now that I was standing here, I wasn't sure I was ready to be here, taking care of traumatized pups. But... I was here now. And having seen the pups, I knew I couldn't leave. Something inside me reached out to them. I needed to do something, anything, for them.

Shane turned away from the doors, his large body slumping in dejection. His silver hair fell into his eyes and I unconsciously reached out to brush it back. I caught myself as my hand rose and instead pushed my own reddish-brown hair back around my ear. Wisps of curls always came loose from my braid and would fly around my face. It was an easy save.

"PTSD?" I wondered aloud. I wasn't sure if I was talking about the pups or the man beside me.

Max nodded. "Some of it, yes. Some of it may just be depression or grieving. We found their parents dead in their den. Probably killed in front of them."

He shook his head, turning to face me, leaning

against the door frame. He was tall, just not as tall as Shane. He had shaved his dark brown hair close on the sides with the top left long to curl over his forehead. His eyes were hazel with strong tints of yellow in them. He was handsome, but I didn't feel any of the attraction I felt towards Shane.

Then again, I haven't felt attracted to anyone since my husband had died six months ago. Not until now.

I glanced up at Shane. He continued to stare out at the pups as if he could will them to thrive.

Looking back at the doctor, I searched for a question. "Are they eating?" Stupid one, Holden, given the untouched bowl of food next to them. My cheeks felt warm. I was off my game.

He shook his head, appearing not to notice. "Not really. It was fine when we had them strapped down and were giving them IV fluids. Now that they are up and moving around, we have been trying to get them to eat for themselves. They won't. They barely drink. We have tried almost everything."

The frustration in his voice caused my heart to ache. It even broke through to Shane, who looked over at Max before turning and walking over to a couch and sitting on one of its arms.

“It is why we invited you here, Dr. Black. You are one of the foremost experts on wolves in the nation. You are also the closest and were available.”

I shivered. I was available only because I was at the end of my sabbatical, extended after my husband’s sudden death. Foremost expert, though? I wasn’t sure they could call me that.

“I understand. What do you want me to do?”

Max shrugged. “Help us figure out why they are not thriving. Help us get them well, so we can reintroduce them into a Pack. Wolf pups need a Pack. These young ones have already gone a while without one. I am not even sure if they can assimilate into a Pack at this point.”

He sounded worried, but I knew why. Lone wolves had a much harder time in the wild. Pups only a few years old? That was basically a death sentence without a Pack to protect them. I just wasn’t sure what I could do since I wasn’t an animal psychologist. These needed more than medical or behavioral help.

Shane leaned forward, clasping his hands, his muscular forearms on his knees. He watched me for a moment and then he sat back up.

"We understand that you were planning to take at least another month on sabbatical. Take it here. Work with the pups. We will pay you well to be their nanny. If you can figure out something that can help us acclimate them, that would be great. If not, then we are no worse off than we were before."

While his words were straightforward and casual, his tone showed the strains of sorrow. And a touch of hope. I wasn't sure how I knew this, but I did. This man cared deeply for these pups. He didn't want to give up on them.

Because of that and the pups themselves, I couldn't walk away. Perhaps it also will be an excellent distraction for me.

I nodded. "Okay. I will become their Wolf Nanny. Here's hoping it helps."

The feeling in the room lightened somewhat. I guess both men thought I might have turned their offer down. They were obviously betting so much on me. What had I gotten myself into?

I glanced out the doors again and noticed that two of the pups were standing, nudging the third.

"Something is wrong." I moved to the door, but Max beat me, pulling open one door and moving swiftly towards an oxygen tank I hadn't even seen sitting next to the den. In the next moment, Shane was holding the smallest pup while Max placed a mask over her nose.

"Come on, Lexi. Breathe for us." Shane cajoled the pup.

Max let out a frustrated groan. "Holden, come hold the mask for me while I get.."

I rushed over and squatted next to them, my hands holding the mask steady.

Max stood and moved to a table nearby that was in a three-sided enclosure in the back corner of the deck. There were several medical devices and vials there. He picked up one vial, read the label and then put it down, moving to another. Holding this one carefully, he pushed in a syringe and drew out some liquid before turning and coming back to us.

Kneeling close to me, he injected the pup and then waited.

The pup started breathing again, shallow breaths at first.

Max exhaled. "Trying to scare us again, Lexi girl?" He smoothed back the reddish fur on the tiny female. The other two pups yipped softly, and Shane lowered her enough so they could sniff her and check her out.

"Hey, kids, your sister is okay. Thanks for the warning." Shane freed one hand to stroke a finger along the pups' heads.

Max stood, taking the empty syringe over to the table before returning with three more. "Might as well give them their antibiotics now. They would need them within a half hour."

He quickly injected the three pups before disposing of the empty syringes.

"What is wrong with her?" My voice was soft. No one had told me to remove the oxygen mask, so I kept it close to her face still.

Max stretched out his back. "Acute respiratory distress syndrome or ARDS. Whatever had happened in that lab had hurt her lungs the most. The other two don't appear to have it. We hoped that it would have cleared by now, but she still has setbacks like this."

Lexi opened her eyes and looked up at me, struggling to come closer. Shane let her go and she scrambled onto my lap. She stared, her eyes a bright green.

"Hello, Lexi. I am Holden." I looked over at the other two who had settled down but still had their eyes on their sister. "The black-red-tan one is..?" I glanced up at Shane.

"That is Soren. The lone male."

I studied the pup. He had an unusual mottled fur and serious gray eyes. He was a little bigger than the sister he was laying besides, and both were larger than little Lexi on my lap.

"So that one, the dark brown one with blue eyes, is Betta?"

He nodded, standing up, the movement fluid and easy.

I patted Lexi before moving her between her brother and sister. The two larger pups nuzzled their sister, sighing as if in relief. Lexi looked up at me and yipped softly. I got the impression she was saying thank you.

"You are very welcome, Lexi. Take a nap. I will be here when you wake."

The pup looked like she was giving me a small grin before snuggling in with her siblings and closing her eyes.

Max and Shane exchanged a look before Shane put out a hand to me.

"I take it you are staying, Dr. Black." It wasn't a question, but I treated it as if it was.

"Yes, I think I am." I wiped my hands off on my pants and walked back into the house.

Chapter 2

Shane

I knew the moment she had arrived. Holden Black. Dr. Holden Black. My wolf sat up and howled.

I studied her. She was leaner than she had been when I had first met her. Almost gaunt. There were lines of grief and sorrow etched on her face now. I knew little about why, just that her husband had died recently. This was how we could get her here so fast, since she had been on sabbatical.

I hadn't realized that it was her.

I thought back to when I had first met Holden. We had both been interns in the animal husbandry lab at college. She had worked in the lab because it was a natural addition to her interest in wolves. I had worked there because it was an easy internship, according to some of my Pack mates that had attended the college before me.

Walking into the room, a young woman sat on the floor, crooning to some lambs she was bottle feeding. The college liked to keep the young lambs in the building as opposed to the barn, to keep them safe. She had a bottle in one hand, and she was talking and laughing softly with one lamb while another bumped her arm. Both had bleated out in panic when they had sensed a predator had entered the room, trying to hide behind her.

They knew a wolf when they saw one.

She had sat there, bits of hay in her red-brown hair, her long braid somewhat unraveled by a lamb having chewed on it. She was sitting cross-legged, and her large gray eyes stared up at me in surprise.

“What…?” She glanced over her shoulder at the two babies cowering behind her.

I snorted, but I didn’t have any desire to hunt

them. I tried to push my wolf deep down inside me, but he wouldn't go. He kept flaring his nose, trying to take in as much of the enticing scent that surrounded her as he could.

I sighed, rolling my eyes at my wolf. This internship wouldn't work if he wouldn't obey.

Mate? He inquired.

Why would you even think about that? We are not ready for a mate! I argued back, surprised. *Go away! I want this internship!*

Mate! He insisted.

I stopped myself from rolling my eyes again. *Okay, okay. I will investigate to see if she is our mate. Back off so the animal babies aren't so afraid of us*!

My wolf grumbled but backed away, taking the sense of being a predator with it. The lambs relaxed and stumbled out to fight for the bottle.

"Sorry, I think it might have been a dog I had played with earlier today. The babies probably smelled it and thought it was still with me. Let me wash my hands and wipe down my clothes." I shrugged cheerily at her, backing away.

I went through the motions of trying to remove the non-existent scent at the sink, before walking over to the pen and thrusting out my hand. "Shane Loren. Intern."

She looked up at me before gracefully standing. The lambs fought over the bottle she had dropped until she laughed and pulled it from the victor's mouth. "One moment, Tam." She scolded.

Her laugh caused my blood to head south to my errant cock. I hoped she didn't notice it pressing against my zipper with my hand hanging outstretched. I shuffled my feet, turning a little away from her, trying to hide my erection. I hoped it wouldn't be as much of a problem as my wolf.

Taking my hand, she shook it vigorously. "Holden Black. The other intern." She dropped it before sitting back down on the floor again to feed the lambs.

"I am surprised they hadn't reacted like this with me. I had been playing with the wolf pups over there." She pointed at the cage on the far side of the room. "Well, I had checked on the pups before I fed the lambs."

I walked over to check on the wolf pups. My wolf

peeked up before settling back down again. These were regular gray wolves, not lycanthropes. While it bothered me to see them in a large cage, I could deal, since we couldn't release these two very young cubs into the wild yet.

"Interesting they have pups." I murmured.

"I had found them when I was out hiking about a week ago. A hunter had killed the mother, and they were crying in their den." Holden answered absently, somehow hearing my comment.

I turned my head to appraise her. "I am surprised they didn't bite you."

Finishing up with the feeding, she stood and stepped over the fence surrounding the lambs.

"I have a way with animals." She shrugged. "And wolves are my favorite. I am studying to become a wolf biologist so I can help bring back these majestic creatures to North America."

Both of my eyebrows shot up. "Wolf Biologist? Is that really a thing?"

She bristled, her hands landing on her hips in defiance. "Yes, it is really a thing. We make little, but we make a difference."

I chuckled. "That sounds like a slogan."

A confused look crossed her face, before she relaxed into a grin. "It does, doesn't it? I should have T-shirts made up."

And with that, I realized that not only was Holden my mate, but she was someone I could like. Perhaps even fall in love with.

"Shane?" Max grabbed my arm.

"Sorry, just had a flashback."

Max gave me a worried look.

"Not a military type of flashback. One from before I had gone. While I was still in college."

I shook my head at him and moved away to greet the research biologist we had invited to look at, and hopefully heal, our pups.

Holden was more subdued than she had been when I had known her before. She was also more experienced. She asked the right questions and didn't just barge in and take control of the situation. It impressed me at how the woman had matured into the person who stood in front of me today. Not that she was a slouch before. No,

Holden Black was both intelligent and articulate.

It was obvious she didn't recognize me, even though she had thrown a puzzled look or two in my direction. I knew I looked very different from when I had known her before, though. I had entered the military with black hair and green eyes but had left it with both changing to silver. Add to that a set of scars, the most visible one running across my chin, and I could hardly recognize myself in a mirror.

I was a different person from the young man who had teased and flirted with her a long time ago.

I sighed. While I had wished she would have remembered me on sight, I was also glad she had not. How could I explain how my hair and eyes had changed so dramatically? Humans may have gotten a streak of gray in their hair, but not more than that. Not have their entire head of hair and their eyes changed to a different color.

I had startled my Pack when I had returned. They knew me on one level, but I had looked so different visually. This had caused a lot of confusion.

Max, though... Max had known.

He had seen this before because he had been a military doctor. He had seen how the killing, bombs, and poisons had impacted lycanthropes even more than it had humans. Yes, we can survive much more than humans could, but it still left its mark on us.

What Max wasn't aware of was that my wolf had considered this woman my mate, the one I wanted to be with forever. He didn't know his best friend had fallen head over heels in love with her, returning from the military to find she had moved on and married while deployed. He didn't know that the wolf didn't care and still wanted her.

I had walked away once, leaving her with her choices. I wasn't sure I would be strong enough to walk away again.

Chapter 3

Holden

I lifted the smallest pup, crooning to her.

"Hey, there, little girl. What's your name? Lexi? Well, hello, Lexi. I am Holden. I am your nanny, at least for now."

Tucking the pup in close to my chest, I walked into the medical area on the deck. Lexi was the last pup I needed to examine.

"First, we need to weigh and measure you, so we know what progress looks like. I know that Dr. Max did this already, but he only knows how to do this like a stern doctor." I loved talking to the little one, and she seemed to appreciate my running commentary. I could see the intelligence in her green eyes as she watched my face.

I placed the pup on the scale, removing my hands from her while I read the display. Picking her back up, I placed her on the table next to it. “Hmmm... you weigh as much as a piglet. You should weigh as much as a lamb at this age, Lexi.” I tried to keep the worry out of my voice. While they were all much too small, the other two pups still were bigger than this little girl.

The pup looked up at me with sad eyes and sneezed, shaking her head.

“Yes, you should, little one.” I reached out and grabbed a tape measure and started taking some measurements. “You are a pipsqueak.” I frowned before looking the tiny pup in the eyes.

“Were you the last one born?” I hated calling an animal a runt, since it seemed so demeaning to them. The last pup born typically was the smallest, according to studies. Lexi looked at me, her little puppy expression serious, and shook her head. Again.

I laughed. “No? You weren’t? Well, little girl, you are perfect, in my mind. I am glad you were not the last born.”

I finished up the measurements and marked them down. “Would you like a treat?” I held out a piece of beef jerky.

The wolf pup sniffed it and then delicately took the dried meat from my fingers. She then waited for me to drop her back down on the ground.

I raised an eyebrow, then picked up the pup and carried her out to the enclosure. I watched as the pup shuffled over to its siblings, dropping the piece of jerky into their food bowl before snuggling in between her brother and sister.

I frowned. That was... very unusual for a wolf. I wondered if I was anthropomorphizing the pups. They were not human. They were predators, wolves, and they didn’t act like humans. Typically. And yet...

This situation traumatized these babies. And appeared to be grieving the loss of their parents. They were not eating or drinking - which meant they were not thriving. This was not good. I went back into the house, turning on my computer to look for suggestions for what I could do next.

After several hours of researching, I only had one partial idea. I yawned, realizing the similarities between what the pups were going through and what I had felt when my husband had died. I had stopped eating while I grieved. I still had problems sleeping. Until everything caught up with me and I would crash for ten or more hours.

Opening the French doors, I went out onto the deck and sat in one of the large rattan chairs, pulling up my feet. The warm evening meant the pups were lying on their blankets outside of their den. I exhaled before reentering the house to collect another set of blankets and a sleeping bag.

Placing the sleeping bag on the deck near the pups, I first covered the sleeping pups with another blanket. I sat down and looked at them, wondering again how best to help them. Yawning, I took off my shoes and wiggled into the bag, folding up another blanket to use as a pillow. Tonight, the nanny would sleep with the kids.

Waking up, I felt the chilly air on my face. It took me a few minutes to remember that I had fallen asleep outside with the pups. On the hardwood floor of the deck.

Looking towards them, I only saw two of them. Where was the small one, Lexi?

I jerked upright, frantically looking around. A small squeak sounded near my hips, inside the bag. I raised the top fabric of the bag and saw the tiny pup peering up at me from the warmth of it.

"Looks like you had a visitor."

I whipped my head around, my breath catching in my chest. Shane stood a few feet away, the sun behind his head so I couldn't see his face.

"Yes, I guess." I stuttered, pushing a hand through my hair, which had unraveled from its braid during the night. I groaned.

Lexi crawled out of the bag and went over to nose her siblings.

"She looks happier." Shane frowned, his tone bewildered.

"How does a wolf pup look happier?" I wondered out loud. I clapped a hand over my mouth and then yawned in the next moment.

Shane squatted down, allowing me to see his face better. He grinned.

"She is interacting with her siblings today." He tilted his head towards the puppies. I watched as Lexi walked around, sniffing Betta and Soren, both who remained lying on their sides. After several minutes of poking them with her nose, she sighed, stepped between them and laid down. The other two shifted, moving closer to her, and all three closed their eyes.

Shane looked back at me. "Think you can entice them to eat?" He held out a fresh bowl of diced meat.

I shrugged. Only one way to tell.

Taking a piece, I shimmied out of the bag and knelt beside the pile of puppies. With the piece in my fingers, I whispered, "Lexi!"

Lexi opened one eye. I held out the piece of meat near the pup's nose. Lexi's nostrils flared, but she didn't move for a few moments. Then she bit down on the piece of meat.

Afraid the pup would do the same as what she had done with the jerky, I waited, holding my breath. This time, though, Lexi chewed the small piece of meat and swallowed.

"Good girl, Lexi!" I turned towards Shane, grinning, but he pushed the bowl closer to my hand. I sat crossed legged and fed Lexi a couple more pieces of meat.

When I tried to feed Betta or Soren, though, neither took the meat, even though both sniffed at it. Lexi then licked their faces, her breath meaty smelling. Waiting a few more minutes and then I offered another piece to Betta. Betta took it, eating it in a few bites, but refused to take any more. Soren wouldn't even take one piece.

"It's progress." Shane replied softly. "None of them had eaten solid food up to now. You encouraged Lexi to eat a little and Betta to eat one bite. Perhaps they will eat more later."

Except they started trembling, rolling over onto their backs, whimpers being squeezed from their little bodies.

"Shane! What is happening?" I looked up at him, my eyes wide with fright.

"Go into the house and call Max, Holden!"

I turned and fled.

Shane

"Go call Max!" I yelled at Holden. I could hear

the pups' voices, not on the Pack bonds, but almost like it was a parallel path in my mind.

Lexi kept repeating, *No Shift! Bad man*! Over and over, her will to remain a wolf pup slipping over her form.

Betta and Soren kept to a refrain of *No shift! Not Safe!* But I could feel another's influence there. A memory that the pups were holding onto. It almost felt like my brother, their father and Alpha.

The pieces came together in my mind. Lycanthrope pups were born in their human form, but these three had been wolf pups both in the lab and since then. First shifts rarely happened until the pups reached puberty, but they had shifted early. I wondered if it was my brother's influence, to keep them safe. Since the pups could handle much more in their wolf's form than they could as a little kid.

I reached down my Pack bond to Max, explaining my theory to him. He agreed, but also realized we needed to keep Holden away while the pups worked for control. She was not aware of our world. He promised to keep her on the phone.

I shifted my body to hide the pups from her as much as I could. I reached out and cast my net for the pups. I knew I had Alpha capabilities. There was a possibility I could bring them into a Pack bond with me, particularly since they had been in one with my brother.

I kept feeling the strands slip away as I reached for them, trying to give the pups some of my resolve to stay as wolves. I could tell they feared shifting, of returning to their human form. I extended again, reaching out with my mind...

Suddenly, the bonds snapped into place. I felt the pups' fear as it poured into me. I closed down my other Pack bonds, not wanting Baron's Pack to feel their anxiousness. These pups did not belong to Baron. These bonds were separate from those, consisting only of them and me.

I poured love and strength into them, striving to calm them down, to ease whatever horror that had forced them into a shift. One by one, the pups relaxed, keeping their wolf form. They fell into a deep sleep as Holden ran back outside.

I wiped a hand over my face, trying to hide the sweat that had been pouring down it just moments before. I sat on my heels and breathed in, turning my face to the sun that was just rising over the horizon.

"How are they? Max is on his way." Holden slid to a stop beside me, staring at the sleeping pups.

I turned to look at her. "They're okay. They got through this, Holden. They are just sleeping now."

She nodded, her hands running over the pups' fur. "Poor babies." Her voice was soft.

I could feel their minds turn towards her, especially Lexi's. Holden represented safety for them. She wasn't lycanthrope. She wasn't part of the lab. She was just pure love to them. I could see them tentatively reaching out to her, as if they could include her in their Pack bonds. I shook my head, smiling. Holden was human, she couldn't be Pack. But I wouldn't stop them from trying. They needed what she represented.

"What is it?" She had caught my brief smile.

"Nothing. Just... it is so ironic that we have had this success — Lexi sleeping with you and eating from your hand. Betta eating one bite. And then they go backwards." I couldn't tell her about the Pack bond they had established with me. Even if it was a step forward. And surprising.

We heard a motorcycle roar into the driveway, and then Max flew out of the house to us. "How are they?"

I looked up at him. "Quiet for now."

Touching on our private connection, I added, *I think I created a bond of some type with them. Soren, Lexi, Betta and I. I can see Lexi reaching out to Holden, but she doesn't realize that Holden is human and cannot be Pack.*

Max nodded, his face thoughtful, before he started examining the three, trying not to disturb their sleep.

Finally, he sat back and looked at us. "You are right. They seem to be okay now. I will give them a more thorough exam later on when they are awake, though."

I nodded, my mind touching on the newly created Pack bonds I had with them. Even if I hadn't wanted to be an Alpha, I guess I was. At least for now.

Chapter 4

Holden

Waking up with three small wolf puppies snuggling against me in my sleeping bag the next morning wasn't surprising. But it was hot. After the scare with them the previous night, it was a straightforward decision for me to sleep out here again to watch over them. I fell asleep soon after Lexi had crawled into my sleeping bag.

All three pups were in the bag with me when I awoke the next morning. Lexi had tucked herself up under my chin, but there was another pup near my feet acting as a foot-warmer, and the third was curled up near the small of my back. Toasty wouldn't even come close to what I was feeling. Sweat was pooling between my breasts and dotting my skin.

None of this mattered, though. I really had to go pee.

I didn't want to disturb them, if I could even figure out how to get out of the bag without kicking one of them, but I needed to go. It was then that Lexi pushed her hind feet into my bladder. Decision made! I now was hoping I would make it in time.

Pushing the pup gently away, I slithered out of the bag and then sprinted for the bathroom. I didn't even notice the coolness of the floor, nor of the early morning air until I had completed my mission. Fall was coming since the temperature seemed to have fallen about ten degrees during the night.

Stepping back into the living room, I teetered between returning to the warm sleeping bag, which meant cuddling more with the pups, or staying up and getting ready for the day.

"Coffee?"

I whirled around, my hand on my chest, gasping.

Shane stood in the kitchen, looking like he had been up for hours already. His silver hair was only a little messy, and his eyes shone in the dim light. Jeans that fit his ass perfectly, and a T-shirt that might have been a size too small completed his look.

I inhaled sharply and then blushed. Taking deep breaths, I centered my thoughts and feelings, trying to ignore how yummy the man looked. Even at this ungodly hour of the morning. I raised a hand to self-consciously brush a few strands of hair away. Darn. I looked like I had been... well, sleeping with puppies. I sighed and gave it up. They didn't hire me for my looks.

"Please."

I guess I was staying in the house now. A quick glance down reassured me that the shorts and tank top I had slept in were decent enough. When was the last time I had shaved my legs? I couldn't remember and just hoped no one could see the hairs that covered them.

As Shane moved out from around the kitchen island, I watched him. It was easy to watch his muscles move in those tight jeans. Delicious.

Darn. I hope I wasn't drooling.

He cleared his throat once, a grin crossing his face.

I coughed, blushing, letting my eyes travel down to his bare feet. I frowned. When had he gotten here? He looked... awake. And yet, it was only six in the morning.

Damn morning people!

"When did you get here?" I blurted out. And then blushed again. "Sorry. I just meant that you weren't here last night when I went to bed. Yet, here you are, barefoot and..."

My voice trailed off as I stared at his feet.

"I doubt I am pregnant."

His chuckle was low and caused something deep inside me to flutter. He handed me a mug of coffee. I stared down at it. He had made it just how I liked it — with lots of cream and sugar. How did he know? I glanced up, startled.

He moved past me towards the couch that faced the French doors. I slowly followed him and sat, realizing that this positioning allowed us to monitor the pups from the comfort of the house.

"N-n-no. I didn't mean that..."

I floundered and then gave up, taking a small sip of coffee. My eyes rolled up in my head. Gods!

This man made the best morning coffee!

"I know." He turned his smile to look out onto the deck. "I arrived this morning. You were outside, sleeping with the pups."

I didn't answer but continued to sip my coffee, enjoying the warmth of the mug in my hands. I pulled my feet up under me and leaned against the armrest, watching both the man and the pups beyond him.

The pups had remained in my sleeping bag after I had left, snuggling closer together inside of it. I hoped they had enough air in there, but I suspected they wanted to stay in the warmth.

Shane turned to look down on me, his silvery eyes amused. "Thank you. I can't believe I had forgotten that wolf pups need to cuddle and sleep together like that. They looked like they enjoyed sleeping with you."

I blushed again, pushing my hair behind my ears. "Thanks. It wasn't a problem. I wanted to be close in case they had another seizure. Besides, I realized that they enjoyed cuddling the other night when Lexi came and slept with me."

I frowned, realizing I had finished the whole mug

of deliciousness. I debated if I should have another cup.

No. I should feed the pups first.

Making my way back to the kitchen, I placed my mug on the counter. Opening the refrigerator door, I stared inside. It was full of bowls of diced meat for the pups. Pulling out one large bowl, I opened the lid and sniffed. Grimacing, I placed that one in the sink and pulled out another. Giving it the sniff test, I closed the fridge door and moved towards the French doors again.

Shane leaned up against the wall next to the doors to the deck, just watching us, his face expressionless.

I moved past him, stepping onto the deck. He followed me but stopped right outside the door while I continued over to the den.

Sitting crossed legged, I lifted a corner of the sleeping bag and peered inside. Yep, three pups cuddling together. Lexi opened one eye to stare at me.

"Lexi! Good morning, girl! Want some breakfast?" I kept my voice soft as I opened the container and took out a small piece of meat, presenting it to the pup. “Come out here if you want this. I don’t want to get our bed dirty.”

The small pup studied me. Just when I thought she wouldn’t move, she carefully rose and took the three steps to leave the confines of the sleeping bag. She lifted the meat from my hand and ate it, a pensive look on her little face. I grabbed another piece and presented it to her. Instead of the pup taking this one, she turned around and yipped at her siblings, who were still lying asleep in the bag.

Betta raised her head, her little nostrils flaring. She rambled out and took the piece, gobbling it down before moving closer to me, trying to stick her nose into the bowl to get more. I placed the bowl in front of her and let the pup eat from it. Betta shoved her head into it and gobbled down the meat.

Soren watched for a moment. Lexi moved back to him before poking him with her nose. He snorted and then stood, joining Betta at the bowl. He looked like he didn’t want to eat, but was soon gobbling as fast as his sister.

“Lexi, you need to eat.” I scolded her. Why did she make sure the other two had first dibs on the meat?

Another bowl slid around my side. “Fresh. For the princess.” Shane’s voice was soft.

I pushed it closer to the pup, and she gave me a canine grin. Before eating, though, she moved towards me to lick my hand in thanks. She then buried her head in the bowl, making up for missed meals.

“Again, thank you, Holden.” Shane’s voice rang with awe.

I shook my head. “Seriously, I did nothing. Just slept with the pups.”

He was squatting behind me, his body warm against my back, his thighs on either side of me. A small shiver traveled down my back.

“We didn’t think to sleep with them, that a night together might help to relieve their feelings of abandonment. But you did.”

I thought about that. Shane knew a lot about wolves, it appeared. I wondered how he had gained this knowledge. I asked him about it when Lexi moved to my lap and looked up at me. Her small body moved in close and her head rubbed up against my shirt.

Her face was clean, having eaten like the princess she was. The other two pups were not as neat and were cleaning themselves after having eaten their whole bowl.

Shane reached around us and grabbed the half-eaten second bowl. "Let me take this in for later. The pups will sleep for a few hours given all the food they had consumed."

He stood, and I missed his warmth. But I dismissed that as I continued to cuddle with Lexi, the young pup squirming around to get comfortable. The other two came over and leaned up against my legs, and soon all three were asleep.

Damn. I wondered if I could get up without disturbing them. I didn't want to sit here in shorts, given it was a little cooler out here. I longed for a hot shower.

Shane grinned as he brought out a few heated blankets. He placed them on the deck outside the den and then lifted two of the pups onto it, wrapping it around them like it was a nest. He left room for Lexi.

"I think you should move her. She is becoming very attached to you, Holden." Laughter sounded in his voice. I wasn't sure what he thought was funny, though.

Lexi whimpered as I placed her into the nest he had made for them. She cuddled up with her siblings, after throwing a one-eyed look of consternation over her shoulder at me.

Shane used a second blanket to close the nest, giving the pups warmth and some privacy. He then stood and held out a hand to me.

Taking it, I felt a jolt run through my body as he lifted me to my feet. I wanted to lean in closer to him, but I wasn't sure why, so I stepped back, dropping his hand.

"Go take a shower. I will watch them until you get back, Holden." He grinned, a smug look on his face before moving over to the deck chairs and settling down. He lifted his coffee mug, looking at me with one brow raised.

I just nodded and headed for the doors. Before going in, I turned. "Thanks, Shane."

He didn't turn around to look at me, but just nodded his response. I turned away and moved towards the bathroom and a much needed shower.

Chapter 5

Shane

I sat in the cool morning air, but I was anything but cold. Leaning up against Holden, while she wore that skimpy outfit had been a test for both my wolf and me. She had felt so wonderful. Smelled fantastic, like the best dark chocolate and rich cinnamon. It surprised me she hadn't noticed how she had affected me.

I shifted in the chair, trying to find a little more room in my pants.

I shouldn't be thinking of her like this. I repeated this to myself again. Think about the pups. Only about the pups.

I hadn't slept at the house last night. In fact, I hadn't slept at all given everything that had happened recently. Wanting to check on the pups and the woman, I had jogged over here early. The sight of her sleeping outside on the deck with the young wolves snuggled in beside her had warmed my heart.

I picked up my phone and moved to the side of the deck, after snapping a quick picture of the pups in their blanket den. I could hear Holden in the bathroom, even from out here, the shower still running.

"Max." My friend picked up after two rings. He sounded sleepy. I glanced at my watch and grimaced. I would be sleepy too at six am, if I had slept.

"Sorry, Max. It's Shane. Holden had gotten the pups to sleep last night. All three of them had cuddled with her in her sleeping bag."

Max grunted. "While that is good news, it is not something that means you should call me this early."

Hearing the water turn off, I turned to look away from the house, lowering my voice a bit.

"Perhaps not, but once they got up, the pups ate about half of a large bowl of meat each."

I moved further into the shadows to make sure I didn't catch a glance of the woman in case she had forgotten to take clothes into the bathroom and had to make a dash for her bedroom.

But that was all I could think about now. Damn.

"Well, that is an improvement." Max sounded a little more awake. "And now?"

I glanced back at the blanketed den. "They are back asleep, and Holden is in the shower."

A long sigh came through the phone. "Go. To. Bed. Shane. That is where all sane people are at this hour of the morning. In fact, take Holden with you and both of you get more sleep. Or not. I don't care."

With that, Max hung up on his end.

I chuckled. Now that Max had mated, he thought everyone should stay in bed as long as possible. Wait until he had his first pups. He will find that six in the morning was not that early with hungry little ones underfoot.

The door open and Holden stepped out. She had

changed into jeans, with a large slouchy sweater over a T-shirt. She also had pulled fuzzy socks over her feet, and she was holding another mug of coffee in her hands. I moved out of the shadows so I wouldn't look like I was hiding. Even if I was.

"There's more coffee. I didn't take it all."

She moved to the chairs that were facing the pup's makeshift den and sat, pulling up her legs so they were curled up under her. She reminded me of a cat, curled with her feet underneath her.

She also looked tired, but I suspected that was because she hadn't had a restful night with the pups lying up against her. Dealing with young pups was tiring for lycanthropes, who had plenty of energy to burn, but humans didn't have that extra well to dip into. Traumatized pups pulled emotional energy from everyone around them, which could be more exhausting.

I glanced at the pups. It looked like they had wrapped the blankets even tighter around themselves. I wondered when they would be hungry again. I hoped that they would eat in a few hours. They were so far below where their weight should be at this point. I wanted to be here for their next feeding. I didn't question what my motivation was for this, though.

"Have we turned the corner with them?" Holden's voice was soft in the morning air.

I shrugged. "Hard to tell. I wish I knew what had happened to them."

The pups weren't talking. It had surprised me I had established Pack bonds with them, and not so surprised they have said nothing to me since then.

She looked at me over her shoulder. "What do you know about their situation?"

I moved to sit beside her.

"We got them out of a lab. They had slaughtered their parents in front of them. The men had taken the pups because they are much easier to manipulate. They did tests on them, given the shaved patches. Best situation? The lab only took blood. Worst? They injected many things that we will never know about into their fragile bodies. Max found only a few residual toxins and medicines in their blood work. Some poisons, though, disperse over time and don't show up in a blood test."

Holden bristled. "I hate this. There is this group that talks about the existence of werewolves.

They capture wolves and experiment on them. Sometimes, they kill healthy animals and then perform autopsies on them to figure out if the wolves are normal or not. Few of the wolves I had found had died naturally. My organization has been looking for clues about them, but they just kill wolves and then disappear. Poof." She raised a balled up hand, flinging her fingers open as she said this.

She didn't see me tense with her words as she continued. "They had approached my boss and were spouting crap and wanting information on wolves, such as how to tell if a wolf was an actual wolf or a werewolf."

I choked silently. Clearing my throat, I asked, "What did he say?"

Holden shot me a wry look. "My boss told them they were crazy and to get the hell out of our building."

I cocked my head. "Do you think werewolves exist?" I held my breath.

Holden tilted her head back to stretch her neck, her eyes closed, her face uplifted. "I don't know. It is possible, but I don't think so. It would be so cool if they did, though. But who are we to disturb them?" She lowered her head and frowned. "I mean, if they were a mix of human and wolf, they still are human and should have all the basic human rights — to privacy and due process. We shouldn't treat them like test subjects. We shouldn't tolerate discrimination in any form."

I exhaled, happy to hear that answer. Particularly with my wolf so interested in her. "I agree."

It was time to change the subject a bit, though. I didn't think it was time to introduce her to lycanthropes. Not yet.

"So, tell me about your research. What were you working on before you went on sabbatical?"

Holden's face lit up. She started telling me about the wolf Pack she had been tracking in the North woods. Mesmerized, I listened to her. If I wasn't half in love with her before, I was now. She had taken the bits of work we had started in college and had expanded it out. She was doing outstanding work.

She had a definite affinity for wolves. Mine snorted in my head. He looked out my eyes again at the woman he had decided was his mate.

Down, boy. I smirked. *The pups come first*.

My wolf huffed at me and then backed away, curling up inside of me.

Chapter 6

Holden

I smiled to myself while I brushed Soren. My morning had been relaxing, talking with Shane about my research. I liked the man.

There was this little niggling thought in the back of my mind, though, that kept telling me I knew him from before, but I couldn't for the life of me remember from where. Sometimes it was his laugh, or a turn of phrase, or even how he would hold his head. If he reminded me of someone, it had to have been someone from my far past. He didn't look like anyone I knew now.

"There, you are! Tangle free and nice and shiny!" I picked up the male pup and placed him on the ground. He made a little hop as if he would scamper away before walking solemnly towards his sisters.

I sighed. I was glad about the progress the pups were making - they were sleeping with me and eating food, but there still was this heavy sadness hanging over them.

I reminded myself that it had only been a few days since I had gotten them to this point. Tonight was the last night I would sleep outside with them, though. The deck just was too uncomfortable and my back ached. I hoped that they could sleep out here on their own.

I moved towards the house, slipping inside as my phone rang. Locating my bag over near the couch, I answered it without looking to see who was calling.

"Good evening, Holden."

I stopped, my heart stuttering.

I hadn't heard from Edward in three months. The last time I had seen him had been at my husband's funeral. Thomas had loved his brother, but something about him just rang every warning bell in my head. It wasn't anything he did or said, but I had caught him watching me from time to time. It was like there was another, more evil person, looking out of those bright blue eyes. And I was the moth he wanted to pin to a poster board.

"Edward. How did you get my number?"

"Blunt and to the point like always, dear sister-in-law." His chuckle sounded forced.

"I am busy, Edward, what do you want?" Instead of picking up my sleeping bag, I dropped onto the couch, wondering if I could just hang up on the man. He would just call me back and keep calling until I blocked him.

Then I felt guilty because, while I had lost my husband, he had lost his brother.

"Well, I haven't seen you since Thomas died. I was wondering how you are. It appears you haven't been at home the last week. When I talked to your boss, he said that you had extended your sabbatical to take on a short research project. Where are you?"

I felt the hairs on the back of my neck rise. I didn't like this man. It felt like he was stalking me. Calling my boss? Checking out my house? I shook my head, my guilt fleeing.

"Edward, I am doing what I need to take care of myself. I loved Thomas. His accident devastated me. I need time."

"Which is why you concern me, Holden. I want nothing to happen to you because of his death. He had told me how he had met you. After you had lost someone else close to you. I am worried. Why don't we meet in town and have coffee? Just talk with me and let me see that you are doing okay."

"I am not in town right now." I grimaced. I hadn't meant to tell him that. I didn't want him to come around now. Or ever. "We can meet when I get back. I will call you then."

I pulled the phone away from my ear and glowered at it. I would call him when hell froze over. I put the phone back to my ear.

There was silence on the other end. I waited. Finally, he sighed and conceded. "Okay, okay. I will give you more time. Just know that I care about you. Thomas was my only brother and when you married him, you became, in my mind, my sister."

I kicked myself. His brother's death would have impacted him as much or even more than me. Perhaps I was reading this all wrong. My voice softened. "Sorry, Edward. I didn't think about that, and I should have. He was your brother for much longer than he was my husband. I will let you know when I am back in town and we can talk."

"I look forward to it. Good night, Holden." He hung up.

I held my phone in my hands, thinking. Thomas had talked little about - or to - his brother during our marriage. Yes, they were family, but they didn't seem to be all that close. Or at least, that was my impression. There were eight years separating them, so they hadn't grown up together. In the six years of my marriage, Edward hadn't visited our house once. We had seen him at their mother's house only a few times.

The call seemed a bit out of character, but nothing he said could account for why I didn't want to meet with him.

My phone vibrated. Opening it, I saw I had received a text from an unknown number. I absently opened it, still thinking about Edward. It took a few minutes for what I was seeing to sink in. Once it had, my breath left me.

It was just a picture. A picture of Thomas' accident. And one I hadn't seen before, not that I had seen many.

It was from close up, close enough I could see the deep indentation where the other car had hit his driver-side door. I could see my husband's face, a look of pure anguish, pain and surprise on it. Blood was pouring down his head, only one blue eye staring out, cloudy with pain. He was facing the person who had taken the picture and I could see the recognition in his face. His mouth was open as if he wanted to say something.

I covered my mouth; the tears falling as I stared frozen at my screen. Thomas had died, not alone, but with someone watching him, taking pictures, not helping him, while he was in extreme pain.

I screamed.

Lexi

I heard the scream, and it thrust me back into

memories of being in that awful place. Hearing the whines of unseen wolves and the screams of humans as the bad people did horrible things. My mind went there immediately, my body trembling. Then I noticed my brother turning his head and looking towards the house.

This was not that place. This was the nice woman. Holden. I ran to the door to the house and pushed against it. She had shut it. I saw that she was lying on the couch, crying, holding her phone tight.

I didn't want to shift, though. Papa had told us to only shift when we were safe. Mama had told us to keep what we were a secret.

And yet, Uncle Shane was here. Was it safe here? I wasn't sure.

I heard a noise behind me and whirled around. Soren pulled a small stool over to me, with Betta pushing from the other side.

Quick. She is crying. Something scared her and we have to help. I urged my siblings to move faster.

They helped me pushed the stool against the glass. I hopped up on it and then stood on my hind legs. The stool was unsteady, but Soren and Betta leaned against it to help steady it. I couldn't reach the handle, though. I was too small.

Let me, Lexi. I am bigger. Soren's solemn voice interrupted me. He always was so serious now. He had taken on the mantle of head of our Pack, except it devastated him he wasn't able to save us.

I was glad we had brought Uncle Shane into our bond. He was a protective wolf. He would be a good Alpha. Our Pack was slowly being built, with him as Alpha and possibly including the woman who was more than human. Who right now needed us.

I jumped down, and he climbed up to replace me. Soren barely reached the handle, scrabbling a little to pull it down.

The door opened, and he lost his balance, since he had a paw on the glass. Betta moved enough to help cushion his fall while I leaped over them both to enter the room.

I jumped up on the couch and sniffed the woman. She shook, her skin clammy, and tears ran down her face. I glanced around, wondering where the danger was. Looking around, I caught a quick glance at her phone. She covered the picture with her hand, but I saw an injured man staring out of it. The man's eyes made me shiver.

Betta and Soren moved closer, their movements tentative. What is it, Lexi? Danger? Betta sounded so lost.

Bad man. Someone hurt someone who looked like Bad Man. I replied, my mental voice a whine.

Poor Holden. Soren's voice dripped with sorrow.

I wasn't sure what to do. The woman stared blankly at nothing, her eyes not seeing us. I didn't know what to do since I wouldn't — couldn't — shift to talk with her. I bumped my head against her hand, but she just kept on crying.

Uncle Shane! Uncle Shane!

Our weak Pack bond with him didn't allow me to know if he heard me.

I pushed in closer, and finally the woman saw me.

"Lexi!" The woman gasped out.

I stretched my head up and licked her face, tasting the salty tears that were there.

We're here. We will help you like you help us. We

are here, Mama Holden.

I knew she couldn't hear me — she was human. And yet, something inside me said that she would understand. That what made her Holden would hear my heart crying for her, trying to console her. Similar to what she has been doing for us.

She dropped her phone and wrapped her arms around me, burying her head into the soft fur on my neck.

"Lexi." She mumbled as she cried.

Shane

I returned to the enclosure that evening and found Holden and the pups on the couch. All three pups were hovering around her, while she slept, tear still falling down her face. Lexi lifted her head and whined at me.

Putting my finger to my lips, I covered the four with a nearby blanket. Soren and Betta were at her feet, so I placed the blanket so they could breathe.

I sat on the coffee table near Holden's head.

"Lexi. What happened?"

The pup whined again and shook her head. I gently touched her, reaching for the Pack bounds, trying to communicate via our fledgling connection.

Lexi?

Uncle?

I exhaled in relief. Touch helped our communication. The bonds must have solidified as the pups healed.

Lexi, do you know what happened?

She screamed. Holden screamed. I think something bad happened. The pup whined and turned away from me, pushing her nose up under the woman's chin.

I sat up and looked around, confused. Noticing Holden's phone was on the floor, half under the couch, I picked it up and held it, thinking.

What happened?

Bad picture on her phone, Uncle Shane. Lexi whined to me.

Her phone? How can I check? Right or left?

Her right hand was peeking out of the blanket, falling to the floor. Picking up her hand, I pressed her thumb to the button. Nothing. Damn.

Lexi shifted a little, exposing Holden's left hand, which had a death grip on the pup. I lifted it, working her fingers out of the pup's fur. Placing the device on the pup, I pushed her index finger down onto the button. It flashed open.

Inch by inch, I pulled her phone out from under her hand, pushing it back into the pup's fur. Holden let out a little sigh as she gripped the pup tighter.

Looking at the screen, my stomach turned, souring.

This was a horrific picture to send to anyone, but given that it was her husband, made it even worse. Someone had been trying to get an emotional response from her and had gotten it. Anger built in me. I fought my wolf for control, given he wanted to hunt and kill whoever had done this to his mate. My mate.

I checked the rest of the statistics. She had received a phone call from a.... Edward Black, just about ten minutes before she had received the picture. Edward Black, Edward.... Black. I knew that her husband's name was Thomas. Who was Edward? A relative?

I stood and moved over to my computer on the island, powering it up. I also checked her other texts and calls. I knew I was violating her privacy, but I couldn't help myself. Anyone who tried to hurt Holden....

My wolf possessiveness showed as he growled in my head. She was ours to protect from harm. This anonymous person who sent the picture had harmed her. My wolf was ready to hunt.

"Wait." I mumbled.

I first searched for Edward Black, but there were too many entries. I then searched for Thomas Black's accident. There, in one article, it mentioned his family; his wife, Holden, and his brother, Edward. That must have been whom she spoke with earlier.

I wondered what they had talked about. She hadn't mentioned the man in the time she had been here. I brought up the surveillance tapes of the cabin and fast-forwarded through the last few hours until I got to where she received the call. Slowing it down, I could only hear her side of the conversation. I hoped that at some point the man would have spoken loud enough that my wolf could hear him.

I heard the wariness in her voice when she had answered her phone. I could see the agitation in her movements as the call continued. I rewound the video and put on my headset, turning up the volume.

There! His responses were faint, but I could catch most of what he said. There wasn't anything one could call suspicious in what he said, but when combined with Holden's responses, I felt the hairs rise on my neck. Something wasn't right there. She didn't seem to like the man. She hadn't mentioned where she was or what she was doing, even though we had said nothing about this project being secret. She was hiding from him.

I sat thinking, letting the video run on until something caught my eye. I rewound it a few minutes and hit play again. She received a picture… I watched her swipe. There was another one. How had I missed it?

I picked up her phone, catching it just as the light on the display dimmed. Still unlocked — good. I glanced at the text message and pulled up the added picture. The one that some asshole had sent to her. It was a close-up of her husband's face. His pleading expression full of pain and despair. As if he had known the person who was taking the picture and was pleading for them to get help for him.

Why had someone simply stood there and taken this picture? I could only think of one reason.

His death was not an accident, but murder.

Someone had rammed Thomas Black's car and then had stood around long enough to take pictures. They now had extended the pain and suffering by sending them to Holden, his wife.

Thomas had seen his murderer. And that murderer was stalking Holden.

No wonder she had broken down.

Someone was hunting my mate.

The question was, though, why now?

Chapter 7

Holden

I woke up, groggy. I was on the couch on my side, with a warm, furry body tucked in against my chest. Very warm. There were two more fuzzy lumps. One at my feet and another lying along my legs. The pups had somehow gotten into the house.

I yawned, stretching out my toes slowly so I wouldn't disturb their sleep. I could hear voices behind me, in the kitchen area, murmuring. Either Shane and Max were here, or someone had put a TV in the kitchen and was watching it.

Lexi lifted her head and looked at me. The pup's emerald green eyes were studying me. I got the feeling that she worried about me, but I wasn't sure why I had that thought.

"I'm okay, Lexi." I whispered, bringing up a hand to rub the pup's back. The voices behind me stopped, as if they had heard my soft whisper.

Before I could wonder about that, Lexi yipped and bumped my chin with her head.

"Ouch." That was louder. I grabbed the pup and wiggled to get away from the other two, trying hard not to push any of them onto the floor.

"Let me take her." Max reached over the back of the couch and grabbed Lexi, the pup whining her protest. "Shhhh, Lexi. Let her get up and settled. She needs to stretch out her back and legs after sleeping for so long."

Shane came around and pushed Betta to the end of the couch and then picked up Soren and placed him next to his sister.

"You can get up now." His voice was a low rumble, sounding strange to me, as if he was hiding his feelings about something.

I sat up and stretched out my legs. Arching my back to bring it back into alignment didn't work as I had hoped. So, I stood and did it again, a soft cracking sound filling the air.

"Well, that must have felt good." Max smiled at me, still holding Lexi, who had turned to watch everyone else.

I gave him a small smile, reaching out for Lexi. "My pup."

Max grinned, handing over the wiggling pup.

I dug my nose into the pup's fur and breathed in deep. This pup smelled like home. It would be tough to leave her. I wondered if it would be okay to keep the pup and then chastised myself. Lexi was still wild. She should return to the forest as part of a Pack. Sadness overcame me, but I pushed it back. It was what it should be.

The pup sighed, looking over towards Shane. He frowned and shook his head, before moving his eyes back up to meet mine.

"What happened?" His voice was still a deep rumble. I wondered what had caused him to want to hide his emotions, except his voice told me he was deeply impacted right now.

I shrugged. How do you tell someone that your brother-in-law was creepy, even if you had no evidence? How do you tell them that someone had sent you a picture of your husband's last moments, that there was a person out there that had seen him hurt but hadn't helped him at all, even when he had begged for help? These men didn't know Thomas. They wouldn't understand.

"Flashback. To when my husband died." That would have to do. I put the pup down on the coffee table, next to Shane. "It's been a while since I've had one. They told me this is just part of the grieving process."

I met Shane's silver eyes and then glanced away. The man didn't look like he believed me, and I hoped he wouldn't ask any more questions about it. I didn't know what to say.

Max interrupted by moving towards the back deck. "Well, we should get these pups outside and fed again. They should eat more." He picked up Soren on his way to the French doors, using one foot to pull the door open wide enough so he could slip through. He stepped out onto the deck. "This is how you little rug rats broke in, isn't it?" He moved outside with the male pup.

Shane stood and took Lexi in one hand and Betta in the other, following his friend.

I exhaled. No interrogation. Good. I turned and

went to the refrigerator, checking the bowls of cut meat. Picking one, I followed the men outside.

The two men were standing with the pups facing them, sitting at their feet, all in a line. The pups stared up at them, contriteness crossing their faces. I couldn't see the men's faces, but it almost looked like the pups were getting a stern talking to. I chuckled, and Lexi swung her head around to look at me.

Shane tensed. I watched the flow of muscle and tendons as his back muscles moved under his T-shirt. Wow. He must work out a lot. I wondered how they would feel under my fingertips, as I smoothed my hands down his back... I shook my head, blushing.

Max turned, catching me ogling his friend, and smirked, taking the bowl of meat from me. Luckily, he said nothing about it.

"I need to add more nutrients to the meat." He dug into his pocket and slipped out a baggie, emptying it into the bowl. He glanced around before shrugging and using his hand to stir the bowl. Handing it back to me, he wiped his hand on his jeans.

"Ewww!" I wrinkled my nose at the bloody

streaks. Max just raised an eyebrow.

"I have had worse on my clothes, believe me. If not me, my wife. Part and parcel of being in the medical field. In the meantime, make them eat. They need both the protein and those extra vitamins I've added." Holding up his hand, still smeared with the juices from the meat, he walked back into the house.

I walked over to the pups and knelt, placing the bowl in front of them. I wasn't sure why I felt the need to come to their defense, but my instincts drove me to do so.

"Leave them alone, Shane." My voice was firm as I shoved one hand against his legs, causing him to stumble a few steps.

Shane jerked in surprise, his eyes searching out mine, but I refused to turn away from the pups in front of me.

Betta and Soren ate, but Lexi sniffed the bowl first and then looked up at me, crinkling her little nose. I grinned and pointed at the bowl.

"Eat, Lexi. You need this."

The pup sighed and then joined her siblings in the meal.

I stood up and looked at the man still standing beside me. His silver eyes met mine. Another feeling of déjà vu passed over me, making me a little dizzy. There was something so familiar....

“A little bossy, aren’t you, Holden?” He grinned at me, before turning and following Max into the house, only pausing at the door to continue.

“Tomorrow, we should play hunting games with them. They need to learn that food isn’t just presented to them.” He disappeared into the house.

I stared after him. He was right. They needed to learn how to hunt. I was sure they would have an easier time learning to hunt than I had trying to figure out Shane.

He seemed like he was friendly one minute. Then he would turn distant before running away the next. I wondered what he was thinking. It was obvious he cared about the pups, but there was something more about this situation he wasn’t saying.

I turned back to watch the pups eat. I was getting some strange vibes here. Like something hid right under the surface and everyone else knew it was there except me.

It felt like I belonged here with the pups and.... Shane. Other times, it was as if I was the outsider. I didn't understand the undertone I felt. While it made sense that these two men had found these pups in a lab where horrendous experiments were being done on them, I couldn't understand why they cared so much about them. They were not scientists. In fact, while Max was a doctor, I wasn't even sure what Shane did.

Movement caught my eye at the corner of the enclosure, disrupting my thoughts. Squinting, I saw a brown and tan wolf push its head through the brush next to the chain-linked fence. I knew it was staring right at me.

I held my breath, my first thought being to protect the pups. I moved between them and the edge of the deck. I wasn't sure why I thought this wolf was here to harm us. But it sure wasn't to say hello.

Glancing at the fence, I hoped that it would slow

down the huge beast. Because it was enormous. I haven't seen a larger wolf, ever.

It growled, its yellowish eyes locking in on mine, its nostrils flaring.

Lexi turned and looked at the wolf before growling her puppy growl back, her ruff on her neck standing straight up. The other two pups looked up at her sound, growling and yipping as they moved to surround me.

I glanced down, surprised. It almost was as if the pups protected me. From a wolf who was several sizes bigger than I was, let alone them. I gasped. It was large enough that it could snap them up in a second.

The links of the fence clanged. Whirling, I watched as the wolf scaled it in seconds. How the heck had it done that? I never heard of wolves in the wild climbing fences like that. They would either go around it or under it, digging to tunnel under the barrier.

It wasn't until it dropped into the enclosure that fear caused my heart to pound.

It was in. In the enclosure. With me and my pups.

The pups went on the defense, with the two female pups taking up guard duty next to me. Soren, though, stopped growling, even though his lips pulled back away from his teeth. He streaked off towards the invading wolf, going on the offensive.

I gasped, knowing that he was way too small compared to it. He would get hurt if I didn't stop him! Before I had taken two steps, though, the young male pup jumped, soaring up and grabbing the larger wolf's nose.

The wolf shook its head, almost in annoyance, and the pup went flying, sliding across the ground to hit up against a rock.

Not even thinking of calling to the two men in the house, I ran to stand between the wild wolf and my pup. That thing hurt my pup. I would not let it kill him.

"Go on! Git! Get out of here!" My voice boomed out; its tone lowered to sound almost like a growl itself. I crouched down a little, giving myself a steadier base, my eyes locked on the wolf. I heard the doors to the deck open, but I didn't acknowledge it. This wolf would attack if I gave it any chance.

"Leave." Shane's voice dropped low, his deep tones causing something to reverberate in my body. I wanted to drop to the ground and grovel, but I fought it and kept standing, protecting the smaller male.

The other wolf, though, dropped its eyes from me, dropping to its belly, a whine coming from it.

"Leave!" Shane's voice roared in my mind, even though it didn't sound like he had increased his volume at all to my ears.

With that, the enormous wolf turned and jumped, almost missing the top of the fence. Its hind feet scrabbled on the links before gaining a foothold and launching over the top, tumbling to the ground on the other side. It ran into the surrounding woods, its tail tucked between its legs, its body close to the ground.

The air still held tension. I resisted my struggle to look at the pup until all trace of the wolf had disappeared. I then moved to check him over, to make sure he was okay. He seemed a little dazed, but nothing appeared broken. I didn't see any blood, either.

Max strode over to me. He must have followed Shane out. "Let me take him, Holden. Check on the other two and Shane."

I glanced at him, bewildered. I understood the other two pups, but Shane?

Looking towards the house, I could almost see the tension radiating from the man. He stood tall, his hands clenched into fists and his eyes glinting in the light. His head was up, and he was glaring into the woods, his own nostrils flaring as he took in deep breaths of air. Something inside of me recognized that this was a dominant male, protecting those under his care. Something inside me thrilled.

I didn't even look down at the two female pups, which were cowering near their den. I just walked straight to Shane, who didn't seem to see me. His focus was on the woods, his eyes shifting over the landscape. And for danger. Step by deliberate step, I went up the stairs, tripping only on the last one. His eyes flicked down to meet mine at the noise.

I shivered. A different man stood in front of me. He was almost like a wild animal himself. Feral. A strange glint shone in his eyes, reminding me of wild wolves I had encountered in the past. He was silent and watching me. I knew he was waiting for something. Some signal from me. I just wasn't sure what.

I reached out and touched him, sliding my hand over his forearm. "Shane."

He growled. Growled! My eyes widened in surprise.

Except that didn't scare me. Instead, it made me want to comfort him.

I grabbed his face with my hands, pulling his head down closer to me, shaking it a little. "Shane, it's okay. The pups are fine. I am fine. The wolf is not here anymore. You made the wolf go."

In my gut, I knew I said the right thing. I suspected that fear for those he protected consumed him.

I heard a weak whine.

Whirling around, I looked in horror. Lexi was down on her side, her little body shaking. Her tongue was out, her pants rapid. Betta was the one whining, poking at her sick sister.

Chapter 8

Shane

Lexi!

I heard Betta's scream in my mind. I had just gotten myself under control, with Holden's help, when I turned to look at the smallest pup. Lexi was on her side on the deck, gasping for breath, her little body shaking as if she was having another seizure.

"Max!"

I pushed Holden to the side, taking two steps to get to the pup. I knelt beside her, running my hands down her body.

"Here, take Soren." Max appeared with the

male pup, shoving him at Holden before he knelt beside me. He checked her over, looking into her eyes and taking her pulse.

"I need to take her to my office." He didn't look at me before getting up and striding over to the medical area. He rummaged around there, before pulling out a vial and a syringe. Coming back, he pulled the liquid and gave her a shot.

I watched as the little pup's shakes eased, but she was still having a problem breathing. Max leaned over her, putting his ear to her chest.

"Damn it!" He looked up at me, his eyes worried. "Collapsed lung. Get your keys, Shane. You drive. I need to monitor her in case she gets worse."

I stood, turning, almost running into Holden.

Holden. We had forgotten about her.

She stood there, her eyes filled with tears, her hand half reaching for Lexi, her other hand clutching Soren against her chest. The little male pup's eyes were crossing. I suspected he had a concussion.

"I have a gun in the kitchen. The middle drawer, next to the sink. Please use it, Holden, in case there is any trouble. In fact, move Betta and Soren into the house with you and lock it until we get back. We need you to take care of these pups while we help Lexi."

Max had already picked up the pup, heading towards the house and the car. Feeling helpless, I looked at her for a moment before walking around her to go get my keys. Running, I met up with Max at the car, sliding into the driver's side.

"Where to?"

He got in beside me, laying the little pup on his lap. He stroked her throat. "My office. I need to take care of her lung first, and then I will need you to force her to shift. She is worse off than I expected. I just hope that shifting will help her body to heal whatever those assholes had done to her."

I nodded, my head jerking once before starting up the car and rolling out of the driveway. I knew that collapsed lungs were dangerous for a pup so young. Heck, it was hard for those of us adults, except the shift would heal them as we moved from form to form. I wasn't sure if it would be the same for Lexi, since she was so young. Most shifters were several years older before they even had their first shift. I suspected my brother had forced them into their wolf form upon the attack, which was part of the reason they hadn't shifted back yet.

My knuckles were white by the time I was breaking for the turn into Max's office. For most everyone around, he was a veterinarian, but for us he was just our doctor. Sarah, his wife and vet technician, was standing at the door, holding it open.

Max slid out of the car and jogged over, passing her. Sarah didn't even wait for me, just followed her husband into the building, her face serious.

I parked and took a deep breath before getting out of the car and following behind them.

Maggie, their receptionist and a submissive wolf in Baron's Pack, sat behind the desk that faced the door.

"Shane, they took her into the back. Natalie's with them. Max stated you should stay out here in the waiting room."

A low growl slipped out of my lips before I shut it off. "Mags, that is Lexi..."

Maggie stood up and walked around the desk,

placing a hand on my arm. A sense of calm crept into me. I felt tired. She pulled me over to a chair, away from the other two people waiting with their pets, staring at me wide-eyed.

Pushing me down into the chair, she leaned a little over me. "Max, Sarah, and Natalie will take care of her, Shane. Let them."

I nodded, rubbing my eyes.

"Would you like something to drink? Water? Coffee?"

Maggie's eyes were empathetic. She was the low wolf in the Pack, and yet, I somehow felt much better, more in control around her. "Water, please."

She stood to walk away, but I grabbed her arm to stall her. "And thanks, Maggie." My voice was harsh with all the emotions I was holding inside.

She nodded before stopping to talk to the other two visitors, smiling at them and explaining about the emergency.

The two older women, one with her cat and the other with a guinea pig, both nodded at what she said. They both opted to stay, even though it was uncertain when Natalie, the other vet, could see them.

Maggie brought me a bottle of water before sitting back down at the desk, her fingers clicking at the computer.

Using our fledging bond, I tried to see if I could tell how Lexi was, but could not. I groaned, sitting back in the chair, my fingers running through my hair.

Max. I could look at via Max. Instead, I chose Sarah, since she was more submissive. Sometimes, the submissive wolves didn't even know I was watching via their eyes. I searched through the Pack bonds and found her, easing into her mind.

Shane. I could hear the resignation in her mental voice.

Please, Sarah. Let me watch. I urged. I could feel the mate bond and Max through her mind. Max was aware I was now there and a little disgruntle I was splitting Sarah's attention.

I watched as they inserted a long tube into Lexi's chest. Max reached out to me then.

Shane, once we have inflated her lung and gotten her oxygenated, we will need you to force the shift. I will send Natalie out to take care of her patients and Sarah will slip you back here. We may have to get her to shift a few times before it heals enough.

I nodded, not answering him. I watched as Lexi started breathing easier, with the tube in her lung helping to inflate it. As her breathing slowed, her eyes fluttered open a little.

"There you are, little one." Max crooned to my niece.

Relief flooded my body. I leaned forward on my chair, dropping my head into my hands I had propped up on my knees. Thank god.

Natalie came in through the door behind the receptionist's desk and smiled at me. "She is now breathing again, Shane. Max will call you back to see her in a few minutes. Meanwhile..." She turned to Maggie and the young woman handed her a folder. "Ms. Whitehill? Can you bring Chubs into Room 1?"

The woman with the Guinea Pig stood up and walked towards the room labeled 1.

"Ms. Loring? I will be with you as soon as I can. Sorry for the wait."

"No worries, Dr. Jackson. Mr. Plumpernickel and I just want that young puppy to be better. We can wait a few more minutes for our annual shots, I am sure."

Natalie smiled and nodded to the older lady. "Thank you." She moved into the room after Ms. Whitehill.

Maggie stood up and waved at me. "Come on, Shane. Come see your pup."

I stood and moved to follow her. Max and Sarah stood next to the table in the other room, Sarah checking the tube, their voices hushed. Max glanced at me as I rushed in.

"She is much better. Let's try to get her to shift. I am leaving the tube in her chest. Then we can remove it and have her shift without it. I am uncertain how many shifts we can force on a young pup, though."

I nodded, walking over to the pup. Touching her, I could feel our bond better.

Sarah threw a towel over the pup, just as I pushed her to shift. The young wolf shifted into a little girl easier than I thought she would.

"I hurt." She whined, her voice rough from

disuse.

"I know, Lexi." Max soothed, while Sarah checked the tube. "I am removing the tube, baby, but then you need to shift to wolf again."

He pulled on the tube, which adhered a little to the skin surrounding it. He waited, watching as Lexi breathed, making sure the lung wouldn't collapse again. Giving me a nod, I wrapped my hand around the back of her neck and pushed her back into her wolf.

The wolf whined a little. I dug my fingers into the fur on her neck and checked her. Exhausted, but better.

Max checked her lungs before gazing up at me. "If we can have her shift at least two more times, that would be ideal. Otherwise, I could work with this."

I nodded and checked in with Lexi. *Two more times or stay here, Lexi?*

The pup shivered and then looked up at me, her green eyes dull. *I want to be better, Uncle Shane. I don't want Holden to worry about me anymore.*

"Okay, Lexi. Max, she wants to go the two

more shifts. She is worried about Holden worrying about her."

Max barked out a laugh. "Silly pup. Let's get you better."

I pushed Lexi as fast as I could, but the last shift back into a pup had been hard on her. She fell asleep while Max was doing his last check.

"Good enough. Let's take her back. I still want to check on Soren."

Chapter 9

Shane

We entered the house, searching for the rest of them. They were on the back deck, Holden sitting on the deck with Soren in her lap and Betta leaning against her. I placed Lexi on the couch and went out to join them.

As soon as I entered the compound, Tessa's scent hit me, reminding me what had started all of this.

Holden leaped to her feet, standing to meet us. Max picked up Soren, taking him to the medical area to check over again.

I was angry. My wolf was livid, wanting to hunt and punish any who would defy my rules.

Why would Tessa come and challenge my mate? She knew we were working with the pups. I could feel my wolf wanting to shift, to follow the female and to discipline her for disturbing my place and my Pack.

My Pack?

I felt Holden touch my arm, and I looked down at her. My wolf was still visible in my eyes. I knew Holden wasn't ready to see this side of me, to learn about lycanthropes, but I couldn't help it. My wolf didn't want to release me yet.

Then she asked about Lexi, while touching my face. Skin to skin. Jostling my humanity back into my head.

My wolf descended, whispering *Mine*.

My nostrils flared to take in her scent. I could deal with the situation now that we had taken care of the threat. Now that Tessa had left us, with her tail between her legs and Lexi was okay.

I wrapped my arms around Holden and shoved my head into the nook between her neck and her shoulder, taking a deep breath. I felt Betta lean against our legs. Looking, I saw the Pack bonds between Holden and the pups forming, still weak, but there. I snorted. They were making her Pack. How was that even possible?

I lifted my head and stared at the woman. "I am sorry. When that bitch attacked you and the pups, my heart stopped. Bitches do that sometimes, and the result never is pretty." My voice was rough, still filled with a touch of my wolf.

Holden's eyes went wide. "That was a female wolf? Damn."

She knew that the females sometimes attacked orphaned pups. It was rare, but it happened. And she had gotten between that bitch and Soren.

And yet…. If it happened again, I bet she would do the same. I knew her. Holden would do anything for these pups.

I studied her. "Yes. Why did you challenge her?"

Holden stepped out of my arms. I didn't want to let her go, but I had no reason to keep holding onto her.

"I would protect these pups. No one and nothing will hurt them, Shane."

She turned to walk into the house, her mind intent on checking on Lexi.

I nodded. She would protect her Pack, and the pups now were Pack for her. How it had happened, I wasn't sure. I just knew I was glad to be a part of her Pack, even if she didn't know it. I wondered, though, how the pups had created the bonds with her.

What had Tessa been doing here? I wasn't permitting the Pack near the compound. My guess is that jealousy drove her, since I had been spending so much time here, with the pups and Holden. But there was no reason for jealousy. We weren't more than acquaintances. Not even friends.

It was unfortunate, but she was becoming a problem I needed to take care of once and for all. She had signaled several times she was interested in being my mate. That would not happen. Ever. Not even before I had met Holden. She was not the person I wanted to spend my life with. My wolf abhorred her. She just had to understand that and deal with it.

I walked out the house, moving into the forest. Once I was far enough away from the house and prying eyes, I shifted. I needed to run and hunt to release the residual tension.

Holden

Soren was okay. The pup had a few scrapes and bruises, but Max had patched him up, putting him down to join his sisters. We fed the three pups a small snack, before encouraging them to go into their den to comfort each other and snuggle.

"I can't believe you got between the pup and that wolf, Holden." Max cleaned up the area he was using as a medical center. "You could have gotten hurt." His tone was even, but his words made it known he was chastising me.

I shrugged. I would not back down on this.

"This wasn't the first time I have worked with aggressive wolves, Max. I have a few tricks I know, and I figured you and Shane were around for added protection. Why did she even come here? The pups didn't act like she was part of their Pack. Why would she want to jump a barrier, just to attack them?"

Max said nothing for a while. Once he finished, he turned towards me. "I don't know. It makes little sense to me either. Shane and I will put deterrents around the outside of the house to keep predators away." He shrugged. "That is the best we can do."

I nodded, looking around. "Where is Shane?"

We slipped inside the house. Max sighed, rubbing his eyes, his shoulders slumped with exhaustion.

"Not sure. Maybe he went for a walk or already started putting out the deterrents. It upset him that the wolf jumped the fence. And you being threatened." He paused, twisting his lips in thought. "It may be best if you sleep in the house tonight. If it makes you feel comfortable, let the pups in, but I would feel better if you weren't outside. I am sure Shane will agree. It took little effort for the wolf to jump the fence. We will have to raise it."

I nodded and followed Max to the front door. "Thanks, Max. For checking over Soren's concussion and helping with the pups."

Max hugged me, startling a yelp from me. Holding my shoulders, he peered into my face.

"No, thank you, Holden. Those pups were dying before you arrived. They are now thriving. Because of you. I weighed Soren today, and he has already gained five pounds. Lexi looks wonderful, still underweight, but she looks like she also gained some muscle and grew a little taller. Betta's coat is smoothing out, not looking as scraggly as it had been."

He gave me another quick hug and slipped out the door, his hand lifted in a wave. "If things keep going well, I will bring my wife here to see them. She has been asking about them and is very curious about you. She is sure Shane is half in love with you."

He left on that comment.

I put my hands into my back pockets and grinned at the door, hearing the doctor get into his car and drive off. Shane? In love with me? I shook my head, turning to go to the kitchen to make my evening meal. Shane reminded me of a friend I had once, another intern. That boy had been different. A good guy, just a little irresponsible. But he was also a nineteen-year-old college student. He had been gorgeous, with dark hair and green eyes. A body that caused me to go home from our internship with wet panties every day he was there. He, though, had been a huge flirt. He had made our time together fun, with so many laughs. He had made learning fun.

And I had fallen in lust with him.

He was not this private man. This solemn man acted as if life had shown him the worst evils, and somehow he had still gotten back up and kept going. His body was lean and toned, as if it had to be to live his life. Not a body builder type of toning, but the toned, muscular body of one who does physical labor might need to have.

Something, though, reminded me of that boy.

I paused, looking down at the counter, wondering what had happened to that boy. I couldn't even remember his name... Sean? John? What had happened to him? I exhaled, the memory filling my mind.

He joined the Marines. They had deployed him the day before our first date. I had waited for him, hoping he would return once he had fulfilled his service, but he hadn't. Letters had trailed off; lives had moved apart.

A sharp pain stabbed my heart. That's right, he had died in the stupid war. A war that he shouldn't even have gone to. How had I forgotten? Perhaps it was because I had fallen into a deep depression once I had heard about his death. A depression full of dreams lost and people gone. It was while I was at this lowest point when I met Thomas. And he had put my shattered emotions back together, piece by piece.

I shook myself mentally, not wanting to delve on that anymore, and opened the refrigerator. I wasn't hungry, but I noticed that someone had left a salad in there. Well, that wasn't for the pups. I pulled it out and searched for some salad dressing, making my own from olive oil and lemon juice when I couldn't find any.

I poured myself a glass of red wine and then moved to the couch and sat down, leaving the lights on dim only in the kitchen. The dinner of animal biologists. Salad and wine. I chuckled to myself.

Lexi pawed at the glass door. Her siblings followed behind her a little slower, Soren looking over his shoulder to check on the forest every few steps.

The pups were wary. And scared. I couldn't leave them out there tonight. I put my dinner on the coffee table and went to open the door.

"Come on in. After today, I think it might be best

if we slept together in here, kids."

The pups yipped and ran for the couch. I watched them jump up onto it. Those scrawny pups lounged over most of the couch. I sighed, grinned, and sat between Lexi and Betta, pushing them to the side. Lexi grinned up at me as she watched her sister get bumped into her brother. Soren just exhaled and moved to the far end, curling up with his nose under his tail.

It will be tight if we tried to sleep here on the couch. Perhaps we should move into the bedroom tonight. The queen-sized bed would be ideal for us.

Chapter 10

Shane

I approached the Pack as a wolf, my ruff standing straight up. I bared my teeth, a silent snarl filling the air.

Tessa cowered behind Miranda, who stood next to Baron. Miranda and Baron were my Alpha pair. I had contacted him so he would be ready for this. He knew I was livid for what she had done.

Tessa was my Alpha's mate's sister, which was why she thought she could do whatever she wanted and wouldn't get disciplined. It was also why she had her eyes on me since she had arrived and became Pack.

I was Baron's second. His Beta.

I growled and then changed, standing naked in front of them and others in the Pack. Nudity was common among us, and I didn't want to waste any time looking for clothes right now.

Baron rolled his eyes and threw a pair of sweats at my chest, which I caught and pulled on.

"What did you think you were doing, Tessa?" My voice was low and deep.

Baron looked at me, confused. He knew I was angry, but he didn't know why. "What's going on, Shane?"

I didn't look at my Alpha, just stalked forward another couple of steps, my eyes glued to the woman cowering behind her Alphas.

"Tessa came to the compound. Which I told everyone not to do. She jumped into the enclosure with the pups and challenged Holden, who is human."

"She was just curious, Shane." Miranda interjected, protecting her sister like always.

"No." My silver eyes went icy cold, causing those who saw them to shiver. Baron was Alpha only because I was not at all interested in challenging him for the Alpha spot. I could take it. I had always been the strongest wolf, even before I had gone off to war. I never wanted to be Alpha. Or at least, not of this Pack.

The others knew. We ignored it and let Baron be Alpha.

I knew, though, it took more than strength to run a Pack. It took wisdom and discipline. Baron's only blind spot was Miranda. And, by association, Miranda's sister.

Miranda was always protecting Tessa. I was so over it. Tessa was not high in our Pack. If Miranda hadn't been the Alpha female, we wouldn't even be here discussing this. They should allow me to punish her for interfering with the pups' progress. Heck, she shouldn't have gone near them at all. It was well over time to discipline this self-serving, egotistical bitch.

Baron eyed the woman in question. "Why did you disobey his command, Tessa? You know Shane had declared it off bounds because of the pups. Those were his brother's pups. He knows best how to bring them into the Pack."

Tessa stood up a little, still staying behind her

sister. "They looked okay to me. That male pup attacked me."

Baron's head swung back to me as Miranda gasped. "Is that true?"

I growled, my wolf wanting to take over and defend my new Pack. "Yes. She jumped into their area and challenged Holden. Soren defended both his space and his sisters. And Holden. Tessa threw him against a tree, knocking him out. Holden got between her and the pup before she could do any more damage. Except she is human and didn't know she was challenging Tessa by not looking away. She was, in her mind, protecting her charge that she was trying to bring back from death. Tessa was wrong. She shouldn't have been there."

Tessa sobbed. "You are never here anymore, Shane. I don't understand what takes up all your time there!"

"My brother's pups!" I roared, my Alpha powers rising with my anger. Many of the wolves went submissive, dropping to their bellies as if they were in wolf form. Those who looked human dropped their eyes, and some fell to their knees.

Tessa dropped to her knees, while her sister

barely stayed standing. Baron dropped his head, shaking it, watching Tessa from the corner of his eyes. I knew I was pushing this issue for him, but he needed to take a stand.

Tessa wouldn't stop.

"I could be their surrogate mother, Shane. We could, between us, take care of them, and make them whole. You don't need that human!"

"Tessa, you know nothing about caring for pups." Max melted into sight from the shadows, his voice stern. He must have followed me, knowing that I was coming here. "Soren has gained five pounds since Holden has been with them. The pups are still wary of other wolves, given how Soren reacted to you. They are not communicating via the Pack bonds yet. They are not acting like Pack with us. Yet, they protected her. They are acting like Pack with her." His gaze traveled to others there. "Holden has created a miracle with those pups. In just a few days. We will introduce them to the Pack gradually, but there is a bond forming between them and her. A bond built on grief."

Guilt flooded me. I don't think I had told Max I had talked with Lexi via our fledging Pack bonds. Of how strong my Pack bonds with the pups were becoming. I wasn't sure why I withheld that information, but I didn't want to bring it up now, with Baron standing here, glowering.

Baron looked at the doctor, his eyes narrowing. "Grief?"

Max nodded. "Holden is grieving for her husband, who had died in the last year in a car accident. The pups are grieving the loss of their parents and whatever had happened in that lab. Like is connecting to like. They are healing."

Tessa foolishly stood up and took a step towards me. "I would like to help. Let me help. Perhaps they would bond with me."

I looked at Baron, my eyes growing darker. Baron knew that I wouldn't allow the other woman near my nieces and nephew, even if she hadn't broken my decree. It was Max who answered her.

"You know nothing about grief, Tessa. You are selfish. You are a spoiled brat. You don't even recognize your place in the Pack."

The words were sharp, cutting straight to the point. Several of the wolves surrounding us nodded. It was an accurate assessment of the Alpha's sister-in-law. The wolf wasn't even beta quality, and yet she schemed and lied her way to things she didn't work for. The Pack knew she was scheming for me, for no other reason except my standing in the Pack. Because I was Beta and could be Alpha if I wanted the position.

Baron knew this. He chose a more diplomatic approach than Max, though.

"No, Tessa. Wait until they introduce us to the pups. Do not go to the compound. Do not challenge Holden. Ever. I will let it go this time, but Shane will determine your punishment if you disobey and go there without permission again."

Baron sounded tired. I wondered if being Alpha was tiring him out, or if it was just dealing with Tessa and the issues she brought to our group. Our Pack was huge. It was an enormous responsibility.

Baron turned and walked into his cabin. Miranda put her hand up to her mouth, turning to follow him.

This was different. It was always the Alpha who meted out punishment. Here, though, he had given it over to me, his Beta. She knew her sister had crossed a line that she may not get back over.

"Shane!" Tessa cried out, taking another step towards me. She was oblivious to what she had done.

Miranda whirled around and grabbed her arm, stopping her. For the first time, she showed her displeasure with her sister. She shook her, Tessa's mouth falling open as she stared back.

I took another step towards them, my voice low. "I will never mate with you, Tessa. Find another wolf. Leave my pups alone. Leave Holden alone. Leave the compound alone. Leave. Us. Alone."

Miranda's eyes went wide. She heard the possession in my voice. She heard the beginnings of a mate bond in how I spoke Holden's name. She pulled her sister behind her, rushing into the cabin, her sister stumbling after her. As they went through the doorway, though, Tessa glared back at me, her face ugly with anger.

"I think you just made an enemy of that one, Shane." Max commented beside me.

"She had no right. She could have done a lot of damage to those pups today."

Max studied me. "And to Holden." He paused and then continued. "Soren is okay. Limited bumps and bruises, but nothing major. Impressive weight gain, though. I thought he looked a little bigger, given how he had attacked, but it was surprising how much he has changed in just a few days. I will weigh and measure the girls tomorrow, but whatever Holden is doing has been a miracle. I think they are thriving because of her."

I nodded, still staring at the cabin door. The rest of the Pack dispersed, melting into the village and the surrounding trees.

Max added softly, "I think the cubs are taking her as their surrogate mother. She appears to be Pack to them, even if she isn't a wolf. I think they will protect her as a Pack would."

Max studied me as I relaxed. I could see the small smile, his suspicions obvious but unspoken. Darn. I wasn't doing a good job hiding my connection to Holden.

I rubbed the back of my neck. "Yes, Holden has been a miracle. I suspect part of it is because the pups can see she is hurting just as much as they are, albeit for a different reason."

Max nodded, not pushing his point.

I turned and melted into the forest. Max knew I needed to shift and run to get rid of some of my angry energy. I hoped to hunt, because I needed to feed my wolf, both physically and mentally.

Chapter 11

Holden

"Holden? Holden! Where are the pups?"

I stretched out under the warm covers. My toes kneaded one furry body while I felt another take a deep yawn around my knees. Lexi just snuggled in closer to my shoulder, her nose warm and moist against my neck.

Huh. That had sounded like Max.

The man burst open the bedroom door, stopping to stare at the scene in my bed.

Neither Max nor Shane had returned last night, and I knew I wouldn't feel comfortable sleeping outside after watching that wolf jump the fence.

Except, when I had moved into the bedroom, the pups had followed me, not allowing me to leave their sight.

Since we were all nervous, I had surrendered, letting them sleep with me in the large bedroom. The plan was for me to use the bed and for them to lie on blankets on the floor. At some point, though, they must have snuggled in on the bed, like they did when we had slept outside.

I yawned. “Sorry, Max. I didn’t feel safe sleeping outside after that wolf had just hopped over the wall. The pups didn’t leave my side at all after the ordeal. So, we all slept in here.”

Max slumped down against the door frame. “Understandable. I just thought someone had taken them.”

I sat up at that. “If you thought that, then I think we must reinforce the fence. Today. Make it taller, harder to get over. I don’t want some mangy dog trying to hurt my babies.”

All three pups looked up at me at that and gave me their weird puppy grins.

I could just imagine Lexi saying something like *She’s ours, Uncle Max* to him.

It startled me to see Max widened his eyes in astonishment. Lexi just gazed at him. I wondered what he thought her look meant.

The pup snorted and Max just shook his head. Huh. Once more, I sensed I was missing something. Something going on right under my nose, and I could sense it, but not quite figure out what it was.

Before I could ask Max, Lexi got up, stretched, and then jumped down to the floor. She wandered out into the living room, her siblings following her on silent feet.

I watched them momentarily before glancing at the clock on the nightstand next to the bed. “Damn it! It’s nine o’clock already. They need their breakfast.”

Max put up a hand. “Let me feed them, Holden. Shower and get dressed. Take your time. I also need to weigh and measure Betta and Lexi. Did Shane come back last night?”

I figured he knew the man hadn’t. I wouldn’t have been nervous if Shane had stayed with us.

I shook my head and disappeared into the attached bathroom.

Max

She's ours, Uncle Max. I always could talk to you and Uncle Shane. We just didn't feel the need to. But you need to protect our new mama.

This shocked me. Lexi had talked to me. And yet, it was not via the bonds of Baron's Pack. This was a different communication path. I wondered if any of them had talked to Shane yet.

Still somewhat in a daze, I made my way into the kitchen. The pups were exploring the living room, after having drank all the water in the large bowls in the kitchen. I opened the doors to the deck so they could go outside if needed, before refilling the water bowls.

Heading out to my car, I got a large bowl of rabbit meat and a small box with holes punched into it. I could hear scratching noises coming from inside the box.

I grinned. This would be a different meal time. The pups needed to learn how to hunt. The extra meat in the bowl was to make sure they got enough nutrition, since they were still catching up on considerable growth right now. But first, they needed to get a taste of live food.

I put the bowl into the fridge and then moved outside onto the deck with the box. All three pups were out there, laying in the sun, near their den.

Putting the box down, I sat on the stairs so I could be closer to the pups.

“Today we will hunt. These are just mice. If they get away, you will have lost a tasty treat. If you catch most of them, then we will move up to more yummy things like rabbit, which is what is in your breakfast this morning. Live rabbit is so much better than day old rabbit, though, kids. I just want to let you know. So, come over here so we can play.”

Soren came over immediately. I figured that the male pup would probably grow up to be an Alpha or Beta, given how quickly he had protected Holden from Tessa. Betta moved a little closer, but Lexi remained where she was, watching her siblings through half-closed eyes.

I grimaced. Well, one pup was better than none. I reached into the box and took out a mouse, dangling it in front of Soren’s mouth. The pup snapped at it, snatching it out of my hand before putting a paw on it and biting it into two.

I jumped. The pup was fast. Definitely leadership quality there. He finished the mouse, spitting out the head before looking expectantly at me for more. I chuckled.

"This one you will have to catch yourself, Soren." I chastised. Pulling out a mouse, I let it loose on the ground in front of the stairs.

Soren was after it in a flash. The mouse scampered into a bush, but the wolf pup flushed it out and almost got it. It ran to his left, but suddenly Betta was there, snapping it up and swallowing it whole. The male pup slid to a stop and growled softly at his sister. I chortled at the smug look Betta wore.

"Good going, Betta! Soren, that is how you work as a Pack. One flushes out the game, the other does the killing. Unfortunately, these are so small that killing means eating."

"Come on, Lexi. Let's get you into this fun game." Holden came out of the house to join us, her feet bare. She cradled a coffee mug in her hands.

Lexi had sat up to watch her siblings hunt, but she

hadn't made her way to the ground yet. Holden gently nudged the pup with her foot. She yipped and then slowly got to her feet and made her way down the stairs.

Holden came and sat on the stairs next to me. "How many do you have? Release two this time?"

I chuckled. "I had ten, but Soren ate the first one when I showed it to him. Snatched it right out of my hand. Betta got the second, which I think made him mad. Let's do two and see who doesn't get one this time."

Holden rolled her eyes. "My bet is on Lexi. She really doesn't seem to be interested."

The pup in question was laying at the bottom of the stairs, watching her siblings.

I grinned evilly, pulling out two mice. I sneakily set them down close to the lazy pup before letting them go.

One mouse ran away from all the wolf pups, while the other ran right underneath her. Lexi leaped a foot in the air before coming down. Betta already chased that mouse, while Soren had gone after the other. Lexi growled and then ran after her sister. Before Betta could turn around, the mouse had changed direction, running directly at Lexi who snapped it up, crunching it down immediately. Betta looked at her sister sadly.

Soren triumphantly came out of the grass with a mouse's tail hanging out of his mouth.

“Poor Betta!” Holden laughed easily.

“Well, she has had one already.” I consoled. “Should we let the rest go? I am okay if some of them win their freedom.”

Holden grinned back. “Yes, lets. Okay, pups, it’s a contest! There are five, no six, mice left. All being let go. If any get away, either you get them later or they have earned their freedom. Ready?”

The pups lined up haphazardly in front of us. Holden pulled her feet up close to her, as I dumped the rest of the mice out of the box. The pups flew around, hunting the rodents.

Holden screamed and jumped up. One mouse had climbed the steps and had run over her toes. Lexi was there in a flash, snapping up the mouse before running back to continue to see how many more she could get.

“Look at you, Ms. Wolf Biologist. Afraid of a tiny mouse.” I just had to tease her.

"Yep. Not even going to deny it." Holden looked around carefully and then decided that she would just retreat for now. "I am going... in there... to get the bowl of meat. Yes, that is it. The bowl." She made a hasty retreat for the house.

I roared in laughter. It had to have been the mouse on her foot that had spooked the woman. I glanced out over the enclosure and saw a silver wolf skulking in the bushes.

"She's afraid of a mouse!" I yelled, letting Shane know what he was missing.

The wolf pups came back and laid down, panting hard.

"So, of the six, how many did you get?" I inquired.

Two. Betta answered first.

One. Soren's answer was sullen.

Two, but Holden caught one for me. Lexi laughed.

Out of the corner of my eye, I saw the silver wolf do a slow blink. Shane didn't seem surprised the pups were talking, but he was that they were talking to me. Interesting. That wolf would have some explaining to do.

"Well, Soren, you had two already. You each got

three, so one got away." I counted.

Uncle Shane got one. Soren pouted. *I chased it towards him, and it escaped through the fence, but he was there and he ate it.*

I laughed harder, holding my stomach. Shane grinned at me from the bushes before slipping away, right before Holden came back out, sneakers on her feet and the large bowl in her hand.

I stood up. "Wait up a minute, Holden. I would like to weigh Betta and Lexi before they gorge themselves on rabbit."

I grabbed Betta and walked over to the outdoor area that I had turned into my medical office. Lexi climbed the stairs and laid down near Holden's feet.

"Silly wolf pup!" Holden smiled down at the pup. "Saving me from a little mouse."

Lexi gave her a look like, *Seriously*? *You were screaming, woman!*

I came back with Betta, dropping her near Lexi before picking her up. "Humph, Lexi. You are much heavier than you were even a few days ago. You must weigh about as much as a bunny rabbit now!"

Lexi grabbed my arm with her teeth and gently bit me, her teeth not breaking the skin. I snickered and moved off to weigh and measure her.

Holden moved over towards the stairs and made her way down them, glancing over her shoulder at the others. She fished out a small piece of rabbit and knelt beside Soren.

"Thank you, Soren, for protecting me yesterday." She gave him the first piece of rabbit, dropping it near his feet. The pup licked her fingers in appreciation and then ate the piece messily.

"What? Playing favorites?" I approached her with Lexi, with Betta tumbling down the stairs after us.

"Thanking my protector from yesterday." Holden put down the bowl of meat and the pups attacked it.

She stood, watching them make a mess.

"As you should." My words were soft but directed solely at her.

Chapter 12

Shane

Something about watching Holden and Max give the pups mice to hunt tugged at my heart. I wished I hadn't run off in anger. I should have been laughing and playing with the pups. Instead, my wolf had taken over, trying to bleed off my anger so I couldn't hurt anyone.

I heard the pups talking to Max. It didn't feel like the Pack bonds I had with them. But they had created a new bond. Perhaps being here, they were creating their own Pack, picking who would be a part of it. I shook my head. I wasn't sure how Packs formed, outside of take-overs. I wondered if this was one way.

It amazed me how protecting Holden was bringing the pups out of the darkness they had been in. And making all of them — Max included — into a family.

I wanted Holden. My wolf wanted Holden. But this went well beyond the fact that she was my mate. Even before, we thought her intelligent, feisty and a lot of fun to be with. None of that had changed. I envied her husband for being able to be with her all of those years. I acknowledged to myself that I had missed her.

I moved back into the forest, going deep enough that I couldn't see the compound. Nor them me. I had noticed signs of Tessa, but they were days old, so she hadn't tried to encroach upon my territory again. At least, not yet.

I had found a few anonymous humans had hiked close to the compound in the last week. While this worried me, I knew people did sometimes wander this way. I would have to keep watch for them going forward, though.

I knew I needed a better fence – much higher, with motion sensors – and perhaps some proximity alarms for further out. This family I was building was important to me and I didn't want anyone to interfere with them. This should be my goal for today.

I moved to where I had cached my clothes and shifted back, dressing quickly. I needed to go into town to the lumber store. And then back to the compound. And Holden. My heart quickened.

I turned and jogged to the road, not sensing or smelling the eyes watching from the bushes.

Holden

Shane returned to the cabin late in the afternoon. His truck was full of fencing and poles to make it harder for a strange predator to jump. He, along with Max and a man called Baron, walked the perimeter, discussing plans to make the fence better.

The pups had moved closer to me when Baron had arrived, their little bodies shaking. I figured they feared most human males now, after their experience in the labs. I stayed beside them during the day. When evening fell, I gave them their dinner and brushed their coats for them, getting them to settle and fall asleep about the time the man left with a wave, his motorcycle loud in the evening air.

Max had gotten a ride back with him.

"So, what is the verdict?" I leaned my head back against the chair I was sitting in and drank in the sight of Shane, who had exited the house, a beer in hand.

Shane took a long drink and my eyes drifted over the long line of his throat, watching him swallow, and then traveled down to his powerful chest. As he lowered the bottle, I looked back up, meeting his silver eyes.

He shrugged. "It will take work, but our friends will help. If we do, we can reinforce it within a few days. We have another friend, Shaz, who can set up proximity alarms and connect them with cameras and to our computers, so we can see who is coming once they trigger the alarms. Electronics, though, will take time to set up."

Lexi, who was still in my lap, snuggled closer. The other two were at my feet. Now that the mouse hunt was over, I could take off my sneakers - at least on the deck. Betta and Soren made excellent feet warmers, even though the night air was temperate.

Shane smiled at me, watching the pups. He moved around in front of me, so I didn't have to continue to crane my head backwards, and leaned against the deck railing. I studied his long legs, wrapped in faded jeans. They should consider the way those jeans hugged his body a dangerous weapon. His biceps bulged as he lifted the bottle to take another sip.

I studied his face, my eyes lighting on the faint scar on his chin. I wondered where he had gotten that. It didn't take away from his looks, though. No, in fact, it just added a depth to them, making him look just a little wild. His silver hair was falling into those magnificent silver eyes that seemed to see right through me.

I wondered how it would feel to have him above me, ready to make love to me, with those eyes so close to my own? What would it feel like to run my hands down his muscular back to his powerful ass and pull him into me?

I felt my core heating, and I shifted in my chair, wondering why these thoughts were getting so strong. He was my boss. I couldn't fuck my employer. I tried to pull myself back into our conversation.

"What about in the meantime? While you are fixing the fence? I think I will bring them into the house at night until I feel reassured that nothing dangerous can get in the yard."

Pups. Think about the pups. And how nothing would to hurt them.

Shane's nostrils flare before a slight smile touched his lips. Then he grimaced. "Sorry about that. I forgot how easy it might be for some of these wolves to jump over the fence into the enclosure. That's my bad. The original plan was the pups go over the fence when they wanted to leave. They shouldn't feel locked in, but they also should feel safe. I will create another exit before they need to leave."

"Like a pet door?" I smirked at him.

"Yes, perhaps a pet door. We need to remember they are wild animals, Holden. They need a Pack, and they will leave the compound."

His reminder hurt. I looked up at him, sadness of the pups leaving one day soon overcoming me. Shadows crossed Shane's face, his expression serious. I didn't want to give up these pups. I didn't want to leave this compound. I didn't want to go back out into the world where my husband didn't exist, and his creepy brother was trying to become something he just wasn't.

I wanted to stay here with Shane and Max and the pups. I felt safe here. But this was just an illusion. I needed to leave, like the pups. Return to my world. Like the wolf that had jumped the fence the other day, nowhere was safe.

My phone rang, and I glanced at the display. Case in point.

I hesitated, wondering if I should answer it, and then scowled. Edward had done nothing to me, I just didn't like him. He made me feel uneasy. Still, he was Thomas's only family. It felt wrong to ignore him. I hit the connect button.

"Hello, Edward. I'm not in town yet. I told you I would call once I returned." There. Taking control from the start.

There was silence on the other end. And then a long sigh.

"Good evening, Holden. I only am contacting you because of something important. The police told me they have a person in custody regarding Thomas's accident. They wanted to talk to you, but they couldn't get in touch with you. So they contacted me."

My heart sped up. They had the person who had killed Thomas in custody? I froze.

"Holden? Holden? Are you still there?"

"Y-y-y-yes. I am here. They do? I don't understand. Why me?"

"I don't know, I am not the police." That was snippy, even for Edward. "Just let me know when you have returned and we can talk with them together."

Lexi raised her head, shivering, her green eyes intent on me.

"Okay, I guess." My voice was soft.

"They would like to talk with us soon, Holden. They can only hold him or her for so long. Something like forty-eight hours, I think."

I nodded and then realized the man couldn't see the movement. "All right. Let me get some things together and I will be there either tonight or tomorrow morning."

"Let me know when you show up. Call me as soon as you are in town and I will pick you up. We will go in together."

I disconnected. What to do? I have to inform Max and Shane and pack some clothes. I looked down at the pups, as all of them were now watching me, their whines quiet. What would I do about the pups? I wasn't ready. I wasn't sure I could deal with this.

Shane shifted. "Trouble?"

I shook myself, clearing my thoughts. "That was Edward. The police have a person in custody. They want to talk to me, I guess. They need me there soon."

Now the shadows crossed his eyes. "Why don't you call the police, Holden? Ask them if you can do what is necessary over the phone."

Betta whined. Shane looked down at the pup and frowned, his lips pursing.

That was a good idea. It might save me the long drive there and back.

I fumbled with my phone and it fell onto Soren. Shane moved forward and picked it up, handing it back to me.

He was right. Something just didn't feel right. Why had it taken a year to find a suspect? While these things happened, what brought the guy to the police's attention? Another accident? Another murder? Why am I necessary?

Was it coincidence that this happened so soon after I had received that photo?

Shane moved uneasily. "Call your contact at the station."

My fingers shook as I punched in the numbers and then hit connect. It rang.

"Detective Bryant, please."

While I was waiting, I watched as Shane did a quick search for accidents or any similar news on his phone.

There was a click. "Hello?" The Detective sounded tired, like he hadn't slept for days.

"Hello, Detective Bryant. This is Holden Black. I heard you had some additional information about who had hit my husband. Yes. No?" My eyes flew up and connected with Shane's. "So, no suspect yet, no reason for me to return? Have you or anyone there at the station called his brother, Edward? Hmmm.... okay, no, that's all right. I must have misunderstood what he had told me. Thank you."

Lexi now was shaking.

Shane sent a quick text, his eyes glued to his phone. “The police have nothing?”

I shook my head, frowning. “Why would Edward tell me that?”

“Why did he want you to return?” Shane glanced up at me and frowned.

I glanced down at the pups. All three were now whining and shaking. Something seemed to have set them off. Almost as if they were having anxiety attacks. My frown deepened as I pulled Lexi up into my arms, my face buried in her fur. I could feel her little heart beating a mile a minute.

A car skidded into the driveway, the door slamming, followed by feet running towards us.

Max burst out the French doors and headed towards us, his face worried.

“Max?” How had he known to come?

Shane, who had dropped to sit on the deck and had pulled Soren and Betta onto his lap, glanced up at me. “I sent him a text when I noticed they were having an issue.”

I nodded, still trying to comfort Lexi.

“What happened?” Max dropped beside my chair and tried to take Lexi. The pup struggled, burying her head against my chest.

“Edward, Thomas's brother, called. I think something about that call triggered the pups. I can’t tell you what, though. Examine Soren or Betta first. I need to comfort Lexi right now.” I couldn’t give up the little girl pup given how much she was shaking.

Max switched to Betta, who was the closest of the two pressed up against Shane. He looked into the pup’s eyes and checked her vitals. “Her heart rate is elevated, she is panting. I would say it is like they are in shock. Possibly an anxiety attack.”

Max pulled over his bag and got out a vial. The whimpers got louder.

“Turn around, Max. I think needles are making their anxiety get worse at this point.” Shane’s voice was tense.

Max turned and filled three syringes. Palming the first, he petted Betta and then injected her with the sedative. He moved around to the other side of Shane and injected Soren.

When he turned back to Lexi, the pup growled at

him, her green eyes locked on the hand that was hiding the syringe.

"Shit."

Shane glanced up after pulling the other two close to his body.

"Holden, hold her head. Lexi, it is just a sedative. It will just help you deal with your bad thoughts. We won't take you from Holden. You will stay with your surrogate mama."

The growls went softer. Max's eyes widened. Given that silent wolves attacked, he wasn't sure if she would let him inject her or if she would attack him. I pulled the pup's head in, ignoring the danger that existed with the crazed pup. Kissing her head, I reassured her. I just knew she wouldn't hurt me, and I doubted she would hurt Max. Still, I hoped he would make it quick.

Max injected her, even as she turned her head to snap at him, bumping my chin.

My teeth clicked together.

Lexi's growl turned to a whine as she turned back to lick my face.

"You okay?" Shane asked, watching closely.

I nodded, rubbing my tongue on my teeth. "She just surprised me."

Max smoothed out the pup's fur. "She is fast, for sure."

Betta and Soren were resting against Shane, while Lexi was cuddling in against me. Their agitation was easing as the medicine took hold, which allowed Shane to relax. Max exhaled, sitting back and pulling Soren out of Shane's lap.

"I wish I knew what set them off." I stared at the two men.

Shane looked up at me before standing, holding Betta in his arms. "Until we do, don't talk to Edward around them. In fact, don't talk to Edward at all. He is lying to you, Holden. I will make a den for them in your bedroom. It is late enough that if they wake tonight, they will want to be near you."

He moved into the house, carrying the other female.

Max stood, Soren in his arms. I envied the ease with which he carried the larger male pup, let alone got up from a sitting position on the deck. He held out his hand and pulled me upright. It wasn't as easy for me to get up holding Lexi. She was small but heavier than she appeared.

We followed Shane into the house and found him putting the finishing touches on a den of blankets for them in my bedroom. We laid the other two pups next to their sister and left, leaving the door open.

Max went into the kitchen and got himself a water bottle out of the fridge. "What is this about Edward Black?"

Shane sat at the breakfast bar, pulling the laptop towards him. "He insisted that Holden return to talk to the police, but when we called the station, they didn't have any new leads, nor did they need to talk to her."

Max held up the water bottle towards me and I nodded. He grabbed another one and brought it over.

"What did he say?"

"He wanted me to let him know when I returned. He said we would go to talk to the police together." I cracked open the bottle and took a long sip.

The two men shared a glance. I looked at them,

puzzled.

“What is your relationship with Thomas's brother?” Shane asked quietly.

I looked bewildered. “I don’t have one. He was at our wedding. He called to talk to Thomas a few times - more often right before his accident. But I don’t know the man. I have felt uneasy talking with him. Like there was something off. Does that make sense?”

Shane and Max shared another glance before Max looked at me and smiled. “I think I know what you mean, Holden. I have met people like that. Sometimes you never know quite what is off with them. But once you do, if you do, everything falls into place and you know why you felt hesitant around them. What it comes down to is this: Trust your instincts.”

Shane pushed a hand through his hair. “Unless you think you should go, it would be best not to leave the pups at this point. I think they would regress. Something triggered them, and I don’t want them to become worse. You can ignore his calls or block them. Either would work, but please don’t talk to him around the pups. He is lying to you and until we can figure out why, it is probably best if you didn't speak with him at all."

I nodded, exhausted.

Chapter 13

Holden

Waking up with the pups in my bed was becoming a routine. I stretched, pushing slightly on the two at my feet.

"Time to get up, pups. We have games set up for this morning."

Lexi raised her head, cocking it slightly to look at me.

I giggled, rubbing the pup's fur.

"Fun games. Seriously, Lexi."

I swung my legs out of bed and made for the bathroom door, coming face to face with Shane, who was just leaving with only a towel around his waist.

Standing just inches away from this man's beautiful body - sculpted abs, tone muscles that moved smoothly under lightly tanned skin — meant my panties instantly went wet. I stared straight ahead, but all that filled my sight was his tanned chest, his pectoral muscles lightly dusted with black hairs.

"Holden." His voice was a soft groan.

Behind me, I heard three thumps as the pups jumped down off the bed and left, but I couldn't focus on them. All I could see was Shane.

Shane put his hands lightly on my waist, his fingers caressing the thin fabric of my pajamas.

I stared up into those silver eyes. They had always seemed both familiar and wrong to me. Like they shouldn't have been silver. I wasn't sure why I believed that.

My eyes went to his collarbone, and I saw the small tattoo there, my gaze sharpening. I reached up and traced the lines - úlfur. Wolf.

I only knew one other person with that tattoo, in that location.

Except... he had green eyes and black hair. And he had gone to war. I had presumed he had died, after an explosion had taken out his entire unit. But... Could it be?

"Shane?" The word was only a breath on my lips.

He saw the question in my eyes. Heard it in my voice.

He nodded, swallowing hard. "I couldn't tell you, Holden. I had returned battered and broken, but I wanted to see you. I needed to see you. By the time I could find you, you had married Thomas. I couldn't disrupt that relationship. I am not that selfish. So I stayed away."

I cupped his cheek softly, my fingers exploring the skin there, traveling along that faint scar line. My body swayed closer to his, his fingers tightening on my waist. "Your eyes. They are not green, though. How...?"

He dropped his head slightly, his gaze flicking to my mouth and then back to my own eyes. "The explosion. I am told that there are times, when someone goes through an extreme trauma like I had, physical attributes can mysteriously change." I could detect a bitterness to his voice. "For me, it was my hair and eyes. They both went silver. The doctors couldn't quite explain it, except to mention that there had been similar cases in the past."

A sob broke free from my lips as I wrapped my arms around him tight, pressing myself close against him. "Shane! I had been so angry when they had told me you had died in action. We had had little time together, before you told me you had to leave, that you were being deployed. But you didn't come home. You didn't return to me."

I couldn't tell him I had felt something for him, something deep. That the news of his death had hit me hard. That I had almost died.

I had been sitting on a bridge in the town I was living in, looking down at the swiftly flowing water, wondering if drowning would be painful, when Thomas had come along. He had talked me down off that wall and then talked me out of the mental abyss that I had fallen into.

Leaning forward, I touched my lips to his skin, tasting him. We had only kissed before his unit had deployed. There hadn't been time. But now... Thomas died some time ago, and we were here together. Could we just pick up things again?

I wondered if there was anyone in his life.

Shane's arms came around me, holding me tight. He kissed the top of my head and rubbed my back. I could feel the dampness of his skin from his shower and smell the slight scent of the coconut scented soap he had used. And I felt his desire for me build against my hip, with only the towel separating us from each other.

A towel. Nakedness. The pups. What was I doing?

I stepped back, my hands dragging on his skin as if they were reluctant to let him go. He released me, his eyes hooded.

"We need to talk. Tell me what happened to you." I cleared my throat. "I would like to know." I scanned his body, this time noting the scars that had marked his frame, including a long, ragged one that ran from one side of his chest around to his belly button. I wanted to touch it, trace it, but I clasped my hands tightly, twisting them and massaging them in front of me.

He smiled, recognizing this was me distancing myself from him. "Okay. Take a shower. Let me get dressed. Perhaps we can have Max start the puppy games so we can talk."

I felt his withdrawal, realizing that I had triggered

it, and mourned his distance. Too much stretched between us. We needed to talk. To figure out where to go next.

I nodded. "Okay. Yes. Mmm... let me take that shower and get dressed. Can you feed the pups?" I knew I was babbling, but I couldn't stop.

Shane reached out and gripped my shoulders. "Holden." He halted, changing whatever he was going to say. "I will feed the pups and talk with Max. Don't worry. Take your time."

I wondered what he had intended to say.

He walked away, leaving so much unsaid between us.

A thought occurred to me. "Why were you in this shower? Why didn't you use the other one?"

He chuckled, stopping at the doorway. "Max and I had jogged over here. He was in that one. I figured I could get a shower before you woke up. Guess I was wrong." He slipped out into the hall, leaving me to think about that.

They had jogged over here. I didn't even know where he lived. His house must be close to the compound, though. Who was this Shane? We would have to take things slow.

Staring after him for a moment, I shook my head before walking into the steamy bathroom. A little of me thrilled. This Shane was my Shane, and he was alive! Without knowing it, I walked with a little bounce in my step, hoping that warfare hadn't changed my friend too much. Because I had missed him terribly.

I rushed through my shower and dressed in jeans and a t-shirt, leaving my feet bare because I was too impatient to pull on socks and find my sneakers. I strolled into the kitchen, searching for Shane.

I found Max.

He looked up at me and grinned. "Good morning, Holden."

"Where's Shane?"

I knew I was being blunt, but I had so many questions.

Max handed me a mug of coffee and came around the kitchen island. "He got a call about something he needed to take care of. He is hoping to return soon. He told me you just realized that he was the boy you knew in college who had gone off to war."

I turned and studied the doctor. This man probably knew how badly the war had hurt my friend.

“Yes, I have. I saw his tattoo. I had always admired that one, and I knew no one else who had that word, úlfur, for a mark.”

Max’s eyes appeared to go yellow for a moment and then returned to his normal brown. I shook my head, wondering if I had seen what I thought I had. Had a wild beast peered out of his eyes? No, this was Max.

Max moved towards me, gesturing at the couch in the living room. He waited until I took a seat in one of the over-sized chairs before he sat near me on the couch.

“Please forgive him for not telling you. He came back a changed man. They had lost him in the war zone. Even his family had thought he had died over there. When he returned, he had more healing to do. When he finally returned and searched for you, he found you happily married. He had returned more withdrawn than he had been before.”

“Shane had been extroverted. He was always pulling me out to bars and parties because he said

I spent too much time in my head." I whispered out loud softly, not knowing the man could hear every word.

Max rubbed a hand over his mouth. "War changes people, Holden. They return different from who they had been. They have trouble coming to peace with what they saw and experienced over there. They grieve for friends they had lost. Once they return, those around them have trouble realizing that the person who returned to them is now different. Shane's hair and eyes changed. His personality also changed. He is a darker, more serious person than he was before. One thing that hadn't changed, though, was his loyalty to his friends and family."

Max stood up, looking behind me. I turned and saw that Shane had entered the room, his eyes moodily watching us. He must have taken care of his task already.

Max kept his eyes on his friend while he continued. "Back already? The pups and I are going to play games. You two talk. This conversation is way overdue. Take your time."

He left through the glass doors, walking out onto the deck and yelling for the three pups, who came running towards him for the game.

I turned back around, staring straight ahead, my hands gripping the arms of the chair. Shane sighed and moved to sit in front of me on the coffee table, his hand trailing down my arm before leaving it as he sat.

“Holden.”

“You should have told me.” I couldn’t meet his eyes. “I had the right to know.”

“And what would you have done? Left Thomas? Rip my heart out again by giving me hope that we could have had something together only to return to him? What would knowing I was alive have done? You thought I was dead. So, I stayed dead to you.”

I sat there, tears gathering in my eyes. Those words, while bitter, were also true. “There were times, even when I was lying beside Thomas, that I missed you so much, Shane. You were more than just an infatuation. You were my friend. I missed my friend.”

He reached out and put a hand on my knee. “And I missed mine. I kept up with you, watching your career grow. I made sure Thomas treated you well. He loved you, Holden, and I think you loved him. I was happy for you. You definitely didn't need my broken self in your life."

I chuckled weakly at that. "We are all broken, Shane. Did you know that I met Thomas when I was contemplating jumping off the bridge near the campus? I waited a week after I found out you were dead. I couldn't see my way to continue on without you. So, I had climbed onto the wall and was staring at the water when Thomas found me. He talked to me, he gave me hope and compassion, he helped me down off that wall. He knew that there was someone else. He knew. He helped me through therapy and the deep well of depression I had fallen into. He waited for me to get well."

I shifted my eyes to look at him, tears now streaming down my face. He was staring back, his own tears falling.

"I..I.. I am glad he was there when I couldn't be." He choked out, rubbing his cheeks briskly.

"He didn't replace you, though, Shane. No one could replace you. I had to learn that there was room in my heart for him, along with you."

He nodded. "Do you think we might start again?

As friends first? Then perhaps as more?" His fear of how I would answer quieted his voice.

I nodded. "I would like that. I think we already have started. Here. With the pups. But you have to tell me what happened to you. Tell me what would cause your eyes and hair to change so drastically that I couldn't recognize you on sight."

His eyes dropped for a second, before lifting to meet mine. "I can, but even now, so many years later, I am trying to piece it all together. Right after the explosion, I couldn't remember much. Some people discovered my body and helped me heal. Saved my life, before returning me to the base. The medics patched me up enough to discharge me with honors before sending me back here. Back home. Max had to do the rest. I am not one hundred percent healed, even now, but I am not as broken as I was when I first returned."

I slid forward, my knees intertwining with his as I pulled him into a hug. "Welcome home, Shane. I have missed you so very much."

He laughed and hugged me back. He turned his head and kissed my cheek, before pulling back slightly.

"Hey, Holden?"

“What?”

“Want to go play with the puppies?”

I laughed; my voice joyful. I stood and rubbed my eyes, before wiping the traces of tears from my cheeks. “Yes. Yes, I do.”

I started for the glass doors, Shane following me.

Chapter 14

Shane

Secret number one was out between us. She knew I had returned and had searched for her. She knew that I was her friend. But there was an even bigger secret still between us, one that had always been between us, that I wasn't sure how to broach with her.

Max had told me that lycanthropes rarely mated with humans, but my wolf always knew that Holden was the one for us. We had seen her in that lab and had sat up and howled. He wanted to claim her before we had left, but I thought we had time.

But we hadn't had time. How can I tell her now?

Now she was on Pack land, she would find out my secret. The pups or Max might show her lycanthropes exist.

I wished that Holden had been a lycanthrope. She would have been a glorious wolf, given how she had jumped in front of Soren when Tessa had come into the compound. In fact, there were many times I had almost forgotten she wasn't a wolf, because her instincts had been the same as one. It was because she had studied them so much, had interacted with them so often, that she had taken on many of the lupine aspects.

I couldn't explain what had changed my hair and eyes. This had been something that I learned was common to lycanthropes, who experienced extreme trauma. A Pack found me soon after the explosion which was the only reason I still lived. That Pack had nursed me back to health. By the time I had returned to my unit, my body had healed, but something had changed my hair and eyes.

I had then discovered that everyone else in my unit had died that day. My Command declared me dead with them. There just hadn't been enough pieces for anyone to identify individuals.

So, they had declared everyone dead and our next of kin had been informed.

They discharged me with honors and I had returned to my Pack, a broken wolf. Max had treated me, both mind and body, and I had recovered enough to rise to become Beta for the Pack. But I had never forgotten Holden, my mate.

And here she was, seeing me again. After she thought I had died.

I walked out to the deck and watched Max, her, and the pups play a game of tag. Max and the pups had slowed things down to a more human speed, allowing Holden to play since there was no way she would have been able to catch them if she had been 'It'. I smiled, watching as she tagged Lexi and then scooted away, her laughter filling the air.

My wolf whined. Holden happy was something we craved. I wasn't sure why my mate was a human, but I decided I didn't care. I liked who she was as a person. She just was it for me.

Betta ran up on the deck, sliding to a stop, her nose touching me, before she ran off. Invitation to play received. I grinned evilly, noticing where Max was standing somewhat closer to the deck, watching Holden and Soren, and leaped.

Max turned his head right before I landed on him.

“It!” I ran off and Max just shook his head.

It didn’t take long before Holden and the pups were flopping to the ground, tired from the game. Max and I sat on the deck stairs, watching them and the forest beyond.

“Why don’t we see if we can bring in a submissive, Shane? A true one, not Tessa. I was thinking perhaps Maggie, since she is so submissive it is almost painful.” Max kept his voice low, not wanting the pups to hear us.

I hesitated. “The pups are higher on any ladder than she is.”

Max nodded. “So, they shouldn’t feel threatened by her coming here. She wouldn’t hurt Holden. In fact, she may just cower in a corner.”

I felt uneasy, protective of the young wolf as her Beta. “Is it okay for her, though? I don’t want her traumatized either, Max.”

“It will be good for her. Maggie is good around humans and puppies. The bitches in the Pack recommend her for new pups. Your pups need to meet other wolves. They need to discover that living in a Pack is not horrible. That other wolves - adult wolves - will not reject them. I think it will be a win-win. Besides, I think Holden will instinctively know she is submissive and will react accordingly. The pups will follow her lead. I sometimes think she is part wolf herself."

I glanced at my friend. Interesting that Max shared my belief about her.

"Do you think...?" Hope peeked through my eyes.

Max shook his head. "I have never heard of a human-wolf hybrid. At least not in the northeast here. If one existed, we would know. Things like that don't stay quiet."

My shoulders slumped. "You are right. It must be her interest in wolves. She has always been interested, so much so that her parents moved into the city to keep her from roaming the woods to search for them. She knows more about our natural brothers than we know."

I glanced over to Holden, who was cuddling the pups. "And she loves pups. She always has."

Max heard the longing in my voice, but ignored it, thank goodness.

I mused over the idea and then agreed. "Okay. Let's invite Maggie here. As a wolf. We will let the pups and Holden know beforehand, so it does not startle them. And we can see what happens."

Max turned away, pulling out his phone. I could sense he had waited until his back was facing me before he grinned. I wasn't sure what he thought was amusing.

Then I frowned. Holden was the piece of a puzzle I couldn't get to fit. I would keep turning it until I figured this out.

Holden

I wasn't sure where Max had found the young female wolf, but he came into the compound via the new back gate, the wolf collared and leashed. I watched her, observing the way the wolf held her head low, eyes toward the ground, her body almost slinking. This was either a very submissive wolf or an abused one.

The pups clustered around me, their stances protective, but they didn't make a move. I knew they were wary after the other female had attacked us. But Max had explained to them he was bringing this wolf, and they seemed to understand him. He vouched for her, explaining what he was doing before he brought her in. And they trusted him.

I just wasn't sure why Max thought telling the pups beforehand made a difference. Except these were very intelligent pups and probably picked up on his tone, if nothing else.

Shane was at our backs, up on the deck, watching silently. I absently noted that he was acting like an Alpha wolf – observing and ready to respond in case anyone was hurt in this exchange. But my focus was mainly on the other wolf.

Max let the female off the leash. She instantly dropped to the ground and whined. My heart stuttered. I slowly moved towards the bitch, ignoring the pups who followed at my side. Sitting down cross-legged in front of her, I held out my hand.

"Does she have a name?" My voice was soft and gentle, since I didn't want to startle her. Lexi leaned against my legs, while Betta dropped to the ground next to me, ready to attack if needed. Soren sat near my back, off to one side. No one could approach me with the pups on the watch.

Max smiled, observing the positions the pups had taken around me.

"Maggie." He kept his voice low.

"Hey, Maggie." I crooned, my hand out in front of me, still.

Maggie looked at my hand uncertainly and whined again. She didn't look like she wanted to be in this position, but she didn't leave either.

"Oh, baby, no one will hurt you here." The truth rang in my voice. This was my territory. This was my decree. I protected everyone within this compound once the pups accepted them.

Maggie responded, sniffing at my outstretched hand and then crawling a little closer so that my hand rested on her head. I rewarded her by scratching behind her ears, and Maggie's whine changed to a groan of pleasure. It wasn't a purr, but it sounded like it would have fulfilled a similar function.

Soren relaxed, dropping to lie down behind us, while Betta flopped to her side while I petted and crooned to the older wolf. Lexi reached out and touched Maggie nose to nose. Maggie moaned and collapsed, dropping her head into my lap. Lexi licked the other wolf's muzzle while I dug my fingers deep into the wolf's fur around her neck, massaging the muscles there.

A few minutes later, I moved to the cage where we had placed the rabbits for hunting. I had felt sorry for the little bunnies, but I knew the pups needed to practice hunting. I let one go.

Soren went straight for it, missing the rabbit when it had leaped up and switched directions on him. Betta tried to predict its turn but got the direction wrong. Lexi just nosed Maggie, as if inviting her to hunt.

Maggie got up with a wolf grin. The wolf shot after the rabbit, foreseeing its turns and caught it, holding it in her mouth. Soren stopped, obviously a little disgruntled that he hadn't caught it, but okay with Maggie having it.

Except Maggie then dropped the rabbit, and the hunt was back on. Lexi now joined in, hunting with her siblings.

I joined the two men on the deck, excited. "She is teaching them how to hunt rabbits! Look, Max! She catches it and releases it when they totally miss where it is going!" I bounced on my toes, my eyes sparkling.

Shane grinned at me as Max laughed. “She is. This was definitely an unexpected benefit.”

When Soren had finally caught the rabbit, he killed it and started to eat. Betta joined him, even though he growled a little.

Lexi, though, trotted over to the cage and pawed it, yipping at me.

“Oh, she wants another one.”

I skipped down off the deck and went to release another rabbit. This time, Lexi caught it, having learned how quickly the rabbit could change directions. Except, after she had killed it, she pulled off a leg and took it to Maggie, offering it to the bitch.

“And with that, you may have a Pack, Shane.” Max turned and entered the house.

Shane

I watched them, a bittersweet look on my face.

Max joined me on the deck, after Holden had left us to release more rabbits for the pups.

"I suspect this is the first time Maggie has been accepted so easily." His voice was soft enough that it didn't carry to either Holden or the wolves in the yard.

I nodded, still watching.

Max continued, frowning. "Holden is good at this. She seems to know how to react to us. How does she know? I have never seen a human so in tune with wolves, Shane. It must be more than study. I think you are right. There is something different about her, something we are missing."

I shrugged. What was there to say? I had already said all this to Max before when he hadn't believed me. I knew Holden though. My wolf wanted the woman. That was what was important to me.

We watched them chase rabbits, Holden releasing them and Maggie teaching the pups how to hunt them. The air was full of Holden's laughter and the pups yips after they had caught one. In my head, I could hear their excited exclamations as they threw themselves into this hunting game. I knew they were letting both me and Max hear their commentaries.

When Lexi had shared her kill with Maggie, Max had to get the last word in.

"And with that, you may have the beginnings of a Pack, Shane." The doctor turned and entered the house.

I stood, shocked. This was my Pack? I was the Pack Alpha? Max implied that Holden was part of the Pack in addition. I could tell by the underlying nuances.

I looked out over the group. Holden was laughing and petting the wolves, giving them encouragement to hunt the rabbits. Maggie was teaching the pups, and the pups were learning from her.

Pack.

I grinned, my mood lifting.

We have to tell Holden about lycanthropes. We also have to introduce her to our dual selves. I wasn't sure how we would swing that, but we would get it done. Somehow.

Pack.

Home.

My wolf huffed, content.

Chapter 15

Holden

I liked the new wolf that Max had brought. The female was an excellent role model for the pups, and Betta had fallen head over heels in love with her, following behind Maggie wherever she went. Soren was still his reserved self, and Lexi remained stuck to my side.

Shane had taken to spending some time alone with Soren, hidden in the far reaches of the compound. I wasn't sure what the males were doing, but Soren always came back tired but more confident. I figured they were doing things that the male pup needed, given his dominance.

I knew this couldn't last.

Max and Shane had left for a meeting earlier in the evening. I was sitting on the deck, Maggie and the pups lying around my feet. It was a perfect evening for a mug of chamomile tea. Maggie had been here every day. Max picked her up in the evenings and dropped her back off every morning.

An enormous wolf appeared outside the fence, near the back wall. It raised its hackles, its teeth shining in the dim light. It looked like the female that had attacked recently, but I wasn't sure. The wolf tried to jump the fence, but fell back, not able to clear the extensions that Shane and Max had added to the walls.

Soren stood, his head lowered in hunting mode, his eyes intent on the intruder. He was silent, showing that he was ready to protect his home. Maggie stood near him, but she appeared more uncertain, shifting back and forth on her paws. Submissive wolves tended not to fight, but she looked like she might make an exception to the rule tonight. They ran, but Maggie hadn't run yet, standing near me, her entire body trembling. Lexi yipped and Betta stood in front of Maggie.

The other wolf tried again to jump into the

enclosure, falling back once more and whining after hitting the ground hard. I wanted to believe that was it. Except there was a swarm of monstrous wolves milling about outside the fence. I had never seen ones this large, and I knew these would jump inside.

But they didn't need to, because dark shadows coalesced into men. Men wearing black clothes with wire cutters in hand that they used to cut large holes into our fence.

Shit!

I took out my phone and called Shane, but the call didn't go through. Glancing at it, I noticed it had no bars. No reception. I frowned. I always had service here. Unless...... these people breaking in had disrupted service. Turning, I ran into the house, only to halt.

Standing at the glass doors was Edward.

I frowned. How had he found me here? Why had he come?

"Edward?"

Lexi twirled around and attacked the man, going for his calves.

"Lexi!"

I ran to grab the pup, but Edward kicked out, aiming at the pup.

"Get off, bitch! Or I will hurt her."

Confused, I shouted, "I am not on...."

Edward kicked out again. His foot hit Lexi in the side. She slid across the deck, hard. Edward grabbed me, pulling me in close with an arm around my neck, his other hand holding my arm tight enough that I was sure I would have a bruise tomorrow.

"Get away, you fucking wolf." Edward growled at the pup. Maggie and Betta pivoted together, eyes going to us. Soren stayed focused on the men in front of us.

"Don't hurt her!" I cried out, my hands going to the arm around my throat, struggling to remove it. Edward's arm was like a steel bar, pressing into my throat, cutting off my breath.

He tightened his hold and leaned down to whisper in my ear.

"I have been looking for you, Holden. If only you had come back into town like a good girl, then I wouldn't have discovered that you have my missing pups. And look, you also brought me an extra female that I can use."

I froze in horror. Edward? Edward had taken the pups and put them into a lab?

"Why me, Edward?" I choked out.

"You are special, Holden, even if you don't realize it. When you and Thomas hadn't been able to have kids, I had told him to get me a sample of your DNA so I could do tests. Imagine my surprise when I discovered that you had lycanthrope DNA. I want to breed you with a male, to see if you can have babies with him, since you couldn't with a pure human like my brother."

Lycanthrope? Pure human? What was he babbling about? Edward must be crazy!

Creak! I watched men peeling open a section of fence, making a hole large enough for the wolf pack to get through.

"Run, Lexi! Take Betta, Maggie and Soren and hide! Don't worry about me, just go!" I screamed until Edward's arm cut off my air supply. I struggled, dark spots dancing in front of my eyes.

"Grab the pups!" He yelled out, dragging me into

the house.

I saw Lexi stand and shake her head. Maggie ran over and pushed her with her nose. She grabbed the dazed pup by her scruff before she and Betta slipped over the side of the deck. I hoped there was somewhere there for them to hide.

I reached down with one hand and punched back into Edward's thigh with the last of my strength. He wasn't as solid as Shane was, but I was at a disadvantage with the lack of oxygen. Edward released me enough for me to suck in enough air to scream out.

"Soren! Hide!"

He clapped a hand over my mouth and dragged me through the house, exiting through the front door and moving towards a car sitting in the driveway. I had a brief glance of Soren slipping over the side of the deck, opposite from where Maggie, Lexi and Betta had gone. A large black wolf was hot on his tail, though. I gasped, trying to take in more air, but couldn't.

Edward drew me over to a dark SUV idling in our driveway. He opened a door and reached inside. I struggled to get away, but the lack of air was causing my eyesight to darken. Tears fell down my face as I saw Edward pull a syringe out of the car.

"Why, Edward?" I whimpered, my voice almost gone.

He stabbed me with the syringe, plunging the liquid into my vein at my neck. As my sight dimmed, I heard the man gloat.

"Thomas was stupid. He didn't realize what he had for a wife. I had to get rid of him. Otherwise, he would never have let me do my experiments. He loved you." This was spat out at me before everything went dark.

Shane

Lexi screamed at me via the Pack bonds.

Intruders! Coming through the fence and.... Uncle Shane! One has Holden! Bad man! It's the Bad Man! He has Holden! Come, save her! Please come save her!

I was in the truck with Max, returning to the compound, when Max jerked to the side of the road.

"Maggie says they are being attacked."

"Lexi says that they have Holden and I think at least one of them also had been in the lab because she called him the Bad Man." I flung the door open, shifting as I hit the ground.

Call the Pack.

Max dialed Baron's number, explaining what little we knew. He shifted and followed me. The Pack was too far away. It would take fifteen minutes until they arrived. Attackers could do significant damage in a short amount of time. We prayed we were close enough to save the pups... and Holden.

I raced through the forest, my mind intent on reaching the compound. Hitting the back of the group, I didn't stop but leaped at a man holding a two-way communicator. I landed on his back, my teeth sinking into his throat. The man fell forward; the communicator dropping out of his hand as he fell to the ground.

I didn't want to kill him, so I shifted my grip to the man's collar and lifted him, slamming his head into the ground. Another wolf attacked me, biting one of my rear legs. I twirled, my teeth snapping. Max came up behind that wolf and grabbed its neck, ripping it out with one bite. I turned towards the man crawling away. I shifted to human and then leaned over the man and slammed his head into the ground, this time knocking him unconscious.

A shot hit me in the left shoulder, and I twirled around, falling. Max jumped the shooter, bringing him down. I got up and ran to my friend, punching the man in the face with my uninjured arm before taking up the gun. I knelt, realizing this was a sniper gun, and I could shoot it using either hand. I had a special way of propping it on my injured arm to help keep it steady.

I took aim and started shooting, both close range and further away. I took out several wolves plus another man before using its scope to look inside the compound.

I watched as a man dragged Holden inside the house and then adjusted to watch the house's entry. The tall man dragged her out of the front door. He kept her in front of him, knowing that she was his shield. That must be Edward. Holding my breath, I waited for a chance to take the man out, trusting Max to worry about the surrounding wolves. I felt the Pack draw near, but they were not close enough yet.

Edward somehow kept Holden against him so I couldn't get a clear shot. Damn it! I didn't want to hurt her. I watched the door open and then saw her slump. What had Edward done? By the way he pushed her into the car, I figured he must have sedated her. When Edward stood up to belt Holden in, I took my shot.

He jerked, the shot hitting the car just inches from his side. Fuck! I needed to get to the firing range more often. The man dove into the car, pushing Holden further in and shutting the door. Damn it! They planned this well. They had a driver waiting in the truck. It roared away, its tires spinning.

I put out a call to my Alpha.

Road. There are at least two men in a car that took Holden.

I felt acknowledgment from Baron. I hacked his bond and heard him command two of the Pack to split off and head for the road. One of them was Splinter, one of the fastest wolves we had. Not only that, he also had bikes stashed at various locations throughout the forest and town. He had the best chance of following them, either as wolf or man.

Max yelped, and I turned back towards him.

Using the gun as a baseball bat, I hit the wolf that had the doctor pinned on the ground. Max rolled over, panting, not rising. I dropped the gun and shifted. My wolf was bigger than the other wolf. And while I didn't like to kill humans, I didn't have the same rules for rogue wolves.

As I started for that wolf, another one hit me in the side. I didn't waver but carried the wolf with me several steps until I got to my original target, grabbing the wolf that had attacked Max by the throat, before dropping and rolling on top of the one on my back. With a flick of my head, I ripped out the throat of one wolf while almost crushing the other. Not taking chances, I rocked several times before rolling back over, bleeding from the bites. Turning my head, I then killed that wolf.

Looking over at Max, I saw that the doctor had risen, but was limping on three legs, the fourth one bleeding and crooked. Max slipped into the compound through the hole where the intruders had opened the fence, huffing.

A large black wolf was standing near the medical hut. It was facing off a smaller, gray and black wolf - Maggie.

Maggie, who was so submissive she was at the

bottom of our Pack, was holding the wolf off from the pups. I passed Max, moving towards the side of the deck, creeping up on them. Maggie's eyes didn't leave the black wolf. She was standing over Soren, who was down on the ground, panting, with Betta beside him.

Where was Lexi?

The black wolf tensed, and I was sure I wouldn't get to him before Maggie got hurt. Except, a small girl of about six peeked out from behind the shelf of medical supplies, raising a gun. She shot the black wolf in its neck. Twice. It yipped once in surprise, its eyes going to the girl, before it stumbled to the deck.

I approached the black, sniffing.

"He's out for the count, Uncle Shane." The little girl, wrapped in a towel, appeared and placed a hand on my head. "I used the tranquilizer gun."

And shot him twice. Max limped up the stairs. *That much will keep him out for a while, if it doesn't kill him.*

I looked up at her, proud. *Good job, Lexi,* I sent via our Pack bond.

The girl wilted. "But they still got Holden, Uncle

Shane! The Bad Man got Holden!" Her voice turned into a wail and Max flinched at the sound.

Lexi, please calm down. The Pack is coming and some of them are tracking her. I will go rescue her and bring her home. I promise. I nosed the little girl, rubbing my massive head against her.

Lexi hiccuped, looking at the other three. "Maggie, thank you." She squatted next to her brother and sister and petted them.

Maggie shifted, moving to the side of the deck to pick up a dress she must have brought here at one point, and slipped it on. "No thanks needed, Lexi. I couldn't let them take you." She knelt beside the little girl and then checked the other two pups over. Looking up, she saw Max, who had laid down near them. "Doctor..."

Max rolled over, unconscious, as Baron and Miranda and others of the Pack appeared. Baron shifted, checking the doctor. "I reckon we are too late for the fight but in time for cleanup."

I huffed and then slipped inside. By the time I had shifted, threw on some clothes, and came back out, adjusting my belt, someone had laid Max out on the deck and was examining his leg. Betta had shifted, turning into a taller girl than Lexi, but not by much. Soren was still in wolf pup form and Miranda was cleaning up his bite wounds, crooning to him about how a brave wolf alpha he was.

"You hurt at all?" Baron's voice was gruff.

I shook my head. The bullet had gone straight through. With me shifting, the wound had healed fast and now was only a dull ache. I could live with it.

"Have you heard in yet from Splinter?" I was impatient for news about Holden.

Baron stood, cracking his neck, before coming over to me. "Yes. He has shifted and is following the truck now on his bike. Boomer grabbed a ride and installed a tracker on the truck when they stopped at a traffic light. They can now follow them from further away."

I snorted. "Boomer, I swear, has the gift of invisibility. He is like a chameleon, able to blend in with his surroundings. It was smart of you to send him with Splinter. We can leave soon."

Baron nodded. "I sent two wolves back to get the trucks. We can go when they arrive." He moved off to go talk with other Pack members.

Lexi walked over to me and hugged my waist. "Uncle Shane?"

I looked down on my niece's head. I brushed her red hair back from her face. "What, Lexi?"

"We need to get Holden back. She is part of our Pack. You also need to tell her about us."

I knelt beside the little girl. "You are right. We will get her back, and I will explain to her about lycanthropes. She arrived to heal you three. You are now well enough to shift. We owe her so much for that, baby. You and Betta and Soren are my family, and I will take care of you always."

I wrapped Lexi in a hug. Betta came over and joined us, wearing a simple shift dress that Maggie must have found for the little girl. I enclosed her in the hug.

A wail came from over near where Miranda was cleaning Soren's leg. The pup lifted his head and then, within moments, a small six-year-old boy was lying on the deck. Miranda reached behind her and handed him shorts and a T-shirt. He pulled them on and limped over to his sisters. Lexi and Betta pulled out of my arms, but I grumbled before pulling all three back in.

“I can hold all three of you peanuts.”

“Well, welcome back, pups.” The strain was clear in Max’s voice. He had shifted, but he was still in a lot of pain. Baron was bandaging his leg, while Maggie searched for an antibiotic shot to give to him.

“Welcome back to the living, Doc.” I grinned at my friend, my arms still clutching the kids.

Two horns honked in the driveway. I gave the pups a squeeze and then stood up.

Lexi panicked. “Where are you going, Uncle Shane?”

I wrapped one arm around her shoulders and then lifted her chin to look her in the eyes. “To go bring Holden home, Lexi. You three can stay as kids or change back to pups, it’s up to you. Maggie, Miranda and Max will stay here with you, along with some of my Pack. The rest are coming with me to get Holden.”

I went to take a step, but Lexi grabbed my shirt, tugging on it to show she wanted to say something more. I leaned down so that my head was level with hers.

“They are not your Pack anymore, Uncle Shane.

Soren and Betta and I are your Pack. Maggie is your Pack. Holden is your Pack. Uncle Baron's Pack is not your Pack."

She moved over to stand near Max, turning to watch us go.

I stared at her in shock until Baron yelled back at me.

"Come on, Shane! The trail is growing cold!"

Turning, I moved through the house and out to the driveway, sliding into the front passenger side of the SUV that Baron now was driving. Doors slammed as Pack members joined the hunt, the cars peeling out of the driveway.

Chapter 16

Holden

I didn't want to leave the darkness, but something was calling to me.

Holden! Holden! Uncle Shane is coming for you.

Lexi! I sobbed. I hoped that the little pup and her siblings were okay, that they had gotten away from Edward. While they were the focus of the others, he had ignored them. Was Edward working with the lab that had taken the pups? Why would he do that?

I groaned, the sedative releasing me to consciousness.

"Wake up, Holden." A sharp slap on my cheek

followed Edward's voice.

I tried to bring my hands up to cover my face but could not move them. Shaking my head from side to side, I opened my eyes, closing them in the bright lights.

"I know you are awake. Open your damn eyes." Edward's voice was mild, even though his words were harsh. I squinted, looking up at the ceiling. He leaned over me and looked down, a distant smile on his face.

"There you are. I was wondering when you would join us. This part is no fun without you aware of what is happening, sweetheart."

I tried to move my legs, but Edward had shackled them down. "What is going on, Edward?" My voice sounded weak, even to me. "Where am I? Why did you tie me down?"

"Oh, dear. Yes. You are in my private lab. I guess I could release you, but I am sure you would just try to escape. Then I would have to hurt you to make you stay here. I don't want to hurt you, Holden. Not until I can see if my theories are correct."

"The pups?" I tried to shake my head enough to

get my hair out of my eyes, but it stayed there. Edward stroked it back and away from my face. I glanced at him, but his face was still distant. He looked more like he was looking at a specimen than a person, let alone his sister-in-law.

"The pups. Yes, well, it appears they got away. The Pack came and killed most of my men." He hesitated and then grinned. "But no matter. As important as they are to my plans, you are the greater prize. Imagine my surprise when I found you there with them? If I had known you were shepherding them, I would have come much better prepared. We would have taken you all." He squatted down, his head disappearing for a minute.

He reappeared with a water bottle. "Here, have a drink. You must be thirsty. I promise, I haven't drugged this, at least not yet." His chuckle was eerie, particularly given that his eyes kept that watchful, intent stare.

He opened the cap and put it near my lips. I took a sip and then a much longer one, spilling liquid down over my cheeks and neck, before he pulled it away from me. "Not too much. Otherwise, you may just throw it back up again."

"What is this about, Edward? Why am I here?"

He strolled away, returning momentarily. He clasped something around one of my legs before releasing that restraint. He then repeated the movement with the other leg, before releasing my hands and helping me to sit up.

I was in a large room. There was a large wooden desk on the far wall. A short couch with matching chairs sat in front of it. Closer to me, it looked more like a lab. There were counters and glass shelving all around me on two sides. There were many medical devices and pharmaceutical vials throughout the area.

I was sitting on a table in the middle of all this.

Rubbing my wrists, I looked down at my legs. A long tether now connected my ankle to the wall. The tether wasn't rope, but looked like a long, thin wire of some sort.

"You didn't know where you were, did you?" The question startled me. I had almost forgotten he was there for a minute, leaning against a counter, out of my immediate reach.

I studied him, puzzled. "I did. I was working with some traumatized pups. My employer had rescued them from a lab… that had been… oh, my god! You had them! You were torturing them and experimenting on those poor pups."

He laughed, shaking his head. Edward looked similar to Thomas except colder. His hair was a tad longer and straighter than his brother's had been, a brown that was almost blond. His eyes were a dirty brown. Thomas had been the better looking one. His hair had been a deep brown and his eyes a light hazel that had green specks floating in them.

I always thought Edward had been trying to compete with Thomas, who was brilliant and easy to love. Not to say that Edward wasn't intelligent, but he concentrated on different, darker things.

"Those pups, as you call them, are lycanthropes, dear Holden. Some consider them an abomination, because they are part wolf and part human. I don't, though. For me, they are the key to what humans should evolve towards, or at least a part of that puzzle. And then, there is you."

"Me? What is special about me?" My mind was whirling. I wasn't sure if the man in front of me was bat-shit crazy or if what he spoke was true. I knew the pups had a high comprehension of

English. But werewolves? That was the stuff of fantasies!

Edward stood up and moved closer, shoving his hands into his front pockets while he studied me. I felt like prey to this man. Perhaps I was, given he had locked me up in this room.

“You come across as human, Holden. You never had a Pack. Don’t seem to need one. And yet, there is lycanthrope DNA in your genetics. How curious. Thomas had given me a sample in the hopes I could find out why you were not conceiving. I told him you needed to fuck a lycanthrope. Not a human like him. I wanted to bring you here to test this, but alas, my brother had other ideas.”

Edward moved around me. I tried to track him with my eyes, not feeling comfortable letting him out of my sight. When he got behind me, though, he leaned in and whispered into my ear.

“He wanted to run away with you. Leave so I couldn’t find you. He thought he was so smart. That I wouldn’t figure it out. So, I arranged for him to die. That picture I sent to you? I had taken it. Thomas had thought at first I would help him. He didn’t know I knew he would leave. I knew my brother. I took the picture and watched him die."

I flung my head back, missing the man's nose as he stood back up straight and walked around to the front of me.

"You. Are. A. Monster." I screamed, tears flowing down my face. I jumped down off the table and tried to grab him, except the tether wasn't long enough for me to reach him. He had planned this well.

Sobbing, I sank to the floor. Edward had killed his own brother. He had tortured and experimented on young wolf pups, who may or may not have had a human side to them. I wasn't sure if I could believe him, but that didn't matter. He believed all of this. He would experiment on me. He had decided I was a lycanthrope, even though it wasn't true. I didn't howl at the moon. I didn't have weird dreams or feelings during a full moon. I didn't shift into a wolf.

I screamed, the sound loud and agonizing. And Edward just laughed.

Shane

I willed the truck to go faster, but Baron wouldn't exceed the speed limit. Not when we knew where Holden was.

We are outside the lab. I think it is the same company that had taken the pups. Splinter reported in via the Pack bonds.

Did you see Holden? I replied before Baron could.

One man carried her in. They had sedated her or knocked her unconscious. This was Boomer.

Baron frowned at me and interjected. *How many men were in the car?*

An uneasiness came across the bond.

Five. Splinter answered. *And ummm... Tessa.*

Baron clamped down on the bonds, shutting me from the rest of the Pack as I lost control of my anger. He held my wolf, refusing to let me shift.

"Shane, we will get Holden back. And punish Tessa. She has now crossed a boundary even Miranda cannot save her from. Execution is what she can hope for if she helped with the pups' kidnapping."

I growled. "She is mine to punish. The pups are my family. Holden is my mate. I get to have the first strike."

"Agreed." The Alpha hesitated and then asked, "Are you in control?"

I knew why he asked. At least one of the lesser males behind us in the car had shifted when I had lost control, and before Baron had closed the pathways. I wasn't sure if I had impacted others back at the compound. I was strong, a definite Alpha in my own rights, and I could impact them all.

I took a few deep breaths, cajoling my wolf for patience. Baron would have to either restrain me physically or banish me from the Pack if he thought he could leave Tessa alive after this. She was dead. You don't sell out your Pack.

I nodded, having given my wolf a promise of justice. He backed away, his essence still close to the surface.

Baron reopened the bonds with Splinter and Boomer.

What happened? Splinter sounded calm, but I could feel the anxiety coming from Boomer.

Shane lost his shit and almost caused most of the Pack to shift when you mentioned Tessa. Baron glanced at me before turning back to the road.

Does it help to know they were dragging her along? She could be a victim. Boomer's voice was tentative.

I froze. Where had Tessa been? Was she still in the Pack bonds? I looked at Baron, my eyes wide.

Baron pulled over as soon as he could, opening his car door. "Terry, drive."

The young man jumped out his side of the car and took the driver's seat, once Baron vacated it. Baron took his, shutting the car door and closing his eyes. Mac, a younger wolf who was making his way up the hierarchy, whined and Baron dug his fingers into the wolf's fur. He had been the one who hadn't been able to resist my anger.

I felt the Alpha sorting through the Pack bonds, searching for Tessa. I left that to him. No use advertising I could command the Pack. I suspected that Baron already had guessed.

"I can't find her." The worry in Baron's voice disturbed me. "It is like she never was part of the Pack." He opened his eyes.

"Ask Miranda." I turned in my seat to look over to my Alpha. "Sibling bonds…."

Baron sighed. “I didn’t want to worry her.” He faced the window, the car traveling fast on the highway again.

Another sigh came moments later. “Miranda cannot feel her either.” Baron looked at me, his look anguished.

I sighed. So, they had cut her from the Pack, isolating her. Was it what she had wanted or was it Edward’s doing, now that he had what he wanted - Holden? I suspected that Tessa’s usefulness was coming to the end, and she might not survive this, despite what she may think. Stupid wolf. All of this because she didn’t understand how Packs worked. I shook my head in disgust.

“Where’s Splinter and Boomer?” I turned my head to talk to Baron.

“About a block away from the lab. The small town doesn’t have many hiding places. Edward planned this well.” Baron’s voice was pensive as he gazed out the window.

“Where’s Shaz?”

“Here.”

The voice came from the far back.

I turned around, glancing into the third row of seats. Shaz, Erin, and Mark sat back there. I sighed in relief, opening the glove box and fiddling with the switches on the electronics there.

"Satellite is on, Shaz. I want the building plans for this lab before we get there. We need a way inside."

"On it already. The Sat will help, though. There are a series of tunnels… I suspect they were older sewer tunnels, or perhaps they were bootlegger tunnels or slave escape routes. They might connect with the building. Give me a few minutes." The man started searching his tablet for the information needed.

I nodded. Shaz was our computer wiz and what we needed right now. I suspected that Erin and Mark would be just as useful. Everyone here was military, except Baron.

Even Mac had experience in the Air Force. He was an exceptional pilot, but he also was at the top of his class in explosives. He wasn't at Boomer's level, but he was better than most.

Baron was a good Alpha because he invited those who had been in the military into his Pack, if the one they had been in had kicked them out when they returned from the war. I didn't understand why a Pack would not take back a wolf who now knew, not only how to kill but also knew how humans fought. It was silly to me, the whole purity thing, but many Packs thought fighting alongside humans contaminated their wolves.

Baron didn't. He knew they were an asset. That was how he had grown his Pack so fast. It was also why no other Pack could come against him. He easily held his territory, which was almost all the states of Vermont and New Hampshire. He also encouraged those who were ready to peel off and start their own Packs to do so, becoming powerful allies.

Baron would give me a good kick in the pants, once this was over. I now had the beginnings of a Pack, with Holden, Maggie, and the pups. I may even get applicants from some others on this rescue mission. Boomer had his eye on Maggie. The adrenaline junkie with the extreme submissive. Perhaps that was a match made in heaven. There had been more shocking ones that had worked well.

"Got it." Shaz's voice came from the back. Both Baron and I turned to look at the man as we took an exit to head to the town.

Shaz looked like he should have turned into a weasel. He was on the shorter side and very thin. He insisted he was just small-boned when teased. His dark hair was always slicked back, and he wore a pencil-thin mustache. His dark eyes were small but fit his thin face, along with his very sharp cheekbones.

His wolf even was on the smaller size, albeit physically fast. And vicious. While Shaz rarely went for the neck kill, he could run or harass a much larger wolf to death. Literally. His endurance was unmatched, and his fur seemed like it was almost as slippery as his hair with all that gel in it.

"It looks like these are old bootlegger tunnels that run up to the Canadian border. There are several entrances - the best would be here outside of the town, or near the library, which is several blocks east of the lab. The lab is on top of a tunnel. While I don't think at first they had connected it, it appears someone, about a hundred years ago, opened a passageway to it. When renovations to the building had occurred, someone had blocked the opening again." Shaz paused.

"Does it look like Edward knows about the tunnel?" I knew that the man was intelligent and doubted he wouldn't have investigated things like this.

"Uncertain." Shaz mumbled.

Baron rolled his head. "We have to proceed as if he knows they are there. Assume they are protecting the tunnel entrances. They also could be a back door escape route for the man. We will have to be careful."

Erin snorted.

Baron turned to stare at her. "Something amusing?"

Erin shrugged. "I've heard about Edward Black. He would have a back door. Several, I am sure. He is hoping that you, our Alpha, would come against him. He views everything like a chess game. So, even if we get the human back, he will disappear and come back later. He is a cockroach."

Chess. I frowned, thinking about that. What pieces were still on the board? Where were our pieces?

I turned around and looked at Erin. "Do you know

who works with him? What sort of security he may have?"

This time, Mark answered. "He loves the mercenary types. I suspect he has hired a few of those troops. I suspect that it won't be easy to get into the lab, given you had gone in for the pups before. The same trick won't work twice with him."

Erin, who had been looking out of the window, flinched. "Terry, pull over."

The man stopped the car.

Erin tapped Baron on the shoulder and pointed. "There's a good example. See that flash up on the light post? That is a camera. They already know we are coming. I don't think this was the first one either. I would have started from the town line with a few cameras and installed more you traveled closer to the lab."

"Shit." Baron pushed his head closer to the window, looking around. "There are at least three cameras here." He banged his forehead on the window and closed his eyes.

I felt him reach out to Splinter and Boomer. I knew what I would do - warn those two about their blown cover. I thought about the tunnels, looking out of my window. We were on the outskirts of town. There were a few shops and stores around here, even though it was residential.

"Shaz. Are the tunnels anywhere near that coffee shop?"

Shaz grunted. "Yep. They are everywhere."

"Erin and Mark? Do you want some coffee? I suggest you going in, taking your time, get some coffee and perhaps something to eat. Give it at least ten minutes before you go looking for the tunnels. Shaz, show Erin how to get into them from there."

Baron stared at me. "What are you planning?"

"If they know the Pack is already here, then he would suspect that I am here. Not sure about you, but you are our Alpha. They have already made Splinter and Boomer. So, we will give them the obvious, with a few unknowns. Let's drop Erin and Mark off and have them come in via the tunnels. We can have Terry, Mac, and Shaz come into the lab a different way, a different tunnel. Splinter and Boomer can retreat and find a third way in, while you and I can go in the front door."

Baron nodded and smiled. "Obvious but devious, Shane." I felt the Alpha in my mind, picking up the rest of the plan. He threw it towards the other two. I saw Splinter lower his head, shaking it. Anyone else might have thought it was in disgust, but the man was chuckling.

There were many ways to play the game, but this one was one of the most vicious.

Chapter 17

Holden

I came awake suddenly, my eyes flying open. I looked around.

Damn! I found myself strapped down on the table again.

I listened carefully, not hearing anyone in the room. Slowly turning my head, I saw that the monitors on the desk were on now, numbers scrolling quickly down the screens. I wasn't close enough to see what they said, so I ignored them.

There were tubes coming out of my arms. I wasn't sure if this was a give-a-toxin or take-blood situation. I didn't feel any different, but then I wasn't sure what he was trying to prove.

When he came over to take a single vial of blood, he smirked at me. Looks like he was giving me something that he thinks will impact me then.

"I see you are finally awake."

I thought back. I wasn't sure what had knocked me unconscious, but knowing this man, he probably gave me a sedative or something. I blinked.

His voice sharpened. "Holden, I am doing what is best for everyone. You have this hidden talent that you are not even aware of. Well, you must unconsciously know it or else you wouldn't have gone into the field you are in. Still, I am curious what else you might have gained from the lycanthropes."

"You are crazy." My throat hurt, and my voice was a rasp. I wondered how long I had been screaming. "Lycanthropes, Edward? Werewolves? Those are things of fantasy books. Werewolves are not real."

He gave me a strange look before walking over to a window on an inside wall. When he lifted the shade, it showed a man squatting in a corner in the glass cage. The man had his head hanging down, his long stringy brown hair covering his face. He wrapped his arms around his very naked body.

Edward hit a button, activating an intercom. "Change, Mercer. Let's show Holden what is walking in the world with us humans. Let's show her that werewolves are real."

He hit another button from the panel on the wall. I watched in horror as the man arched his back, his head flinging back to hit the wall behind him, his mouth opening in a silent scream. And then it wasn't silent, but was a high-pitched scream that changed to a howl as the man sprouted fur and his face elongated into a muzzle. Claws popped from his fingertips and he hunched down, his bones cracking as his body changed into a gray and brown wolf.

Tears leaking from my eyes, I watched, giving the man... wolf.... my attention and respect. The wolf's yellow eyes swung to me and we shared a look. Somehow, I knew he would help me if we had the opportunity. This man was.... Not Pack. No, he didn't want to be Pack. Still, he was like Shane. He was an Alpha.

My eyes widened in realization. Shane was an Alpha? I was thinking like a wolf! What was Edward giving me? My eyes flew to the bag attached to the IV.

"Ah, you realized that you are not as human as you thought you were, did you?" Edward moved back into my line of sight. I had forgotten he was there for a moment, with the horror of Mercer's forced shift. "Well, you weren't human before this, but I am testing if Mercer's blood will help you shift."

He puttered around, almost talking to himself. "Some books say that Lycanthropy is a virus, easily caught. Others say it is something in the blood or saliva. I know because of those pups that it can breed true."

I gasped. What pups? Mine? Was this the lab my pups had escaped from? The one that had tortured Lexi, Betta, and Soren?

Bad man, Bad man, Bad man.

The chant that Lexi had screamed suddenly made sense. Edward was the one, the one who hurt my pups.

Lexi! I screamed in my mind.

Holden? A quiet, young girl's voice came back.

Lexi? Startled, I pushed out again.

Holden! Wait a minute.... The voice faded and then came back. *Mama Holden, Uncle Shane is on his way to you. Wait for him. Tell her, Uncle Shane!*

Holden? This time the voice was male. It came with a feeling of safety and home.

What is going on, Shane? How can I... I shook my head, before stopping and looking around frantically for Edward. He was at the glass cage, watching Mercer change back to human, the change agonizingly slow.

Hold on, love. We are coming. His voice in my head sounded soothing, confident. I wondered if this was all a hallucination, talking to Lexi and Shane in my mind. It couldn't be real. But in case it was....

Shane, there is another wolf caught here. Edward is torturing him, making him change from man to wolf and back slowly. He called him Mercer.

Anger flowed into my mind. *We will get him out when we come for you...* And then his presence disappeared, the silence filling my mind with loneliness.

I looked back at Edward. He was staring at me, his hand on another switch.

"What were you doing, Holden? Have you developed the Pack bonds already? It is too soon. You are not wolf enough. So, what were you doing?" His voice ended in almost a scream.

"Hallucinating." I coughed. My throat was so dry. "I just watched a person change to a wolf and back. That cannot be true."

Edward studied me. I was telling the truth, just not the whole truth. But he shouldn't be able to tell. Unless.... My eyes widened again. "Have you tried to infect yourself, Edward? Just like you are doing with me?"

He snorted, standing up tall. "Of course, silly hybrid. Mercer's blood is potent. He is older than he looks. It hasn't worked, though. Yes, I hear murmurs of words sometimes when I am around the lycanthropes. I am a little stronger, but that could be from my training. I don't think they can infect me, unfortunately, the way those silly fantasy authors state. But no worries. I will figure it out and become a hybrid."

He walked towards me, watching intently. "But you, Holden, are not human to start with. You already, somehow, have lycanthrope genes. Perhaps even was born a hybrid. I should be able to kick-start you and your wolf genes. Perhaps in studying you, I can find out how to change myself."

"Why are you doing this? Why do you want to be a wolf, Edward?" I could hardly breathe, my anxiety spiking.

"Why? Well, because I would then be a superhuman. Unstoppable. Except I wouldn't hide like the Packs do now. No, people would listen to me. And then there is the money. There are organizations out there who would pay me millions to figure this out, Holden. Even more if I could give them a live human-wolf hybrid that could breed more like her." His eyes glinted evilly at me.

"How do you know they won't just capture you and use you like you are using me and Mercer? How do you know they won't treat all of us like monsters?"

"Because I will hold all the cards. They won't know how to change more people. They want a super-military group. They want power. Without me, they will not get it." Edward raised an eyebrow at me.

"And Thomas? Was your brother in your way?" My voice caught, remembering how moralistic my husband had been. He would not have gone along with this plan.

"Thomas has always been an uptight prig. Once he realized what I wanted with your blood, that it was not about your lack of fertility..." He paused, thinking. "Well, your lack of fertility with him was a factor. You were different enough from him I don't think you could breed with him. Perhaps some humans, but I suspect you can only get pregnant from breeding with a lycanthrope. Similar to Mercer."

I struggled against my bonds. Edward was crazier than I had originally thought.

"I am not having sex with a man I don't even know, Edward!"

He laughed; the sound humorless. "You will do whatever I say you will do, Holden. I can make you want to mate with him. Once I force you into heat, you will want the closest male to you. Any lycanthrope male."

Shane! I screamed in my mind.

Chapter 18

Shane

Uncle Shane! Lexi's voice screamed in my mind, using the Pack bonds. Talk to Holden! Mama Holden, Uncle Shane is on his way to you. Wait for him. Tell her, Uncle Shane!

I froze. We had already dropped off Shaz, Terry and Mac to rendezvous with Splinter and Boomer in a park a little way from the coffee shop. Shaz would direct them to a tunnel to the east of the one that Mark and Erin would enter.

Somehow, Lexi had connected with Holden.

"Holden." Wonder filled my voice. *Holden*? I continued via the Pack bonds.

Baron gave me a sharp glance and then tapped into my mind via a private pathway. He watched me and Lexi talk with Holden somehow.

When I finished, I stared at my Alpha.

“Holden must be wolf.” Baron stated the obvious.

I nodded and then my face tightened. “Which is even more reason to get her away from that son of a bitch.”

“Agreed.”

We pulled up at the lab and parked the SUV, hurrying towards the front door of the lab. We were going in the front, since we knew Edward would expect us.

Entering the door, we stopped short. There were two men, both dressed in black, and armed to the hilt. Tessa was standing in front of them, her arms crossed over her chest, her hip popped out on one side. Her smile when she saw us was spine-chilling and smug.

Dragged in? This didn’t look like she was here under duress.

Baron ignored the men and looked at her. “Why, Tessa?”

I knew her sister would be very disappointed in her. Miranda had sponsored Tessa, so that the woman could join the Pack. She had sheltered her sister since her parents had passed away. Yet, here she was, violating the most important law — betraying the Pack.

The men behind her had semi-automatic guns pointed at the floor. They exuded a confidence that they could shoot us first. They probably were using silver bullets, but these guns themselves shouted to me that these men either were ex-Navy Seals or mercenaries. Or want-to-be mercenaries, which could be worse.

"I was always lesser than everyone else, Baron." The woman sneered at us. "Miranda is your mate, second only to you in the Pack. But I wasn't good enough for anyone else. Not even you, Shane! Not even after you came back broken from the war. Heck, you even treat Maggie better than you do me, and she is so submissive she would pee if you looked at her wrong!"

I shot out a thought on a personal bond line, hoping it would get to Shaz. *Tessa's here. Working with Edward.*

I had noticed that one man had pointed a device

at Baron, that looked like a remote of some sort. Tessa had a similar device in her pocket. Perhaps this was how she was invisible in the Pack bonds. Which meant they knew Baron was the Alpha and could communicate with his Pack via the Pack bonds. They were making sure he wouldn't be able to reach anyone. They got that information from Tessa.

Neither she nor they knew that I could take over as Alpha able to communicate with both Baron's Pack and my fledgling one.

Shaz replied, *Roger*.

I had noticed that there were steam or wire shafts above the tunnels. I hoped that Shaz would redirect the rest to use those, since I couldn't trust that Tessa hadn't heard some of what we had said before we had locked down the Pack communication. We had done that so that Miranda couldn't learn how involved in this mess her sister was. Shutting down, though, also shut out Tessa from learning what the full plan was, which would be in our favor right.

Tessa was still venting at Baron.

"Edward promised me I could now rise in the Pack, perhaps even become Alpha. He promised that I could breed the next super soldiers for him. That I would be greater than you all." She spit this out at us, her hatred obvious. "I heard you, Baron. There are men waiting for your Pack in the tunnels. We will capture them, just as we have you, and cage you all like the dogs you are. You will fuck me for priveledges . You will want to fuck me after Edward gives you the aphrodisiac. You won't even know it is not Miranda. And I will take pictures to show her how her precious Alpha has cheated on her."

I wanted to roll my eyes. Tessa didn't know how mate bonds worked. Baron wouldn't be able to mate with anyone other than Miranda. Someone could force an artificial attraction to another female, but when he went to mate, his wolf wouldn't allow it to happen.

A hissing sound came from over near one man and he picked up a communicator, listening to it. I strained to listen in but couldn't hear anything because Tessa was still screaming at Baron.

"I will have your Pack. I will have your Pack bonds. And you will be a whored-out dog in a cage!"

Baron listened, a tired look crossing his face. "Is

that what you think will happen, Tessa? Do you think you can trust Edward, a man who killed his own brother, just to forward his own agenda?"

Tessa stopped; her mouth gaping open and her eyes wide. "H-h-he didn't..."

Baron nodded. "He did. He wanted Holden, whom you gave him on a platter. We don't know why he wanted her, but I can guarantee you won't mean as much to him now. He probably will put you into a cage along with us."

One man next to her sighed and then slipped a syringe out of a chest pocket. He struck Tessa's neck, pushing in the plunger with one movement. He caught her as she dropped, her eyes wide with surprise.

"I hoped that she could have just walked down to the lab before we had to do this, but you had to tell her now." He shook his head in disgust as he threw her over his shoulder in a firefighter's hold. Two more men came out of a nearby door, both with their weapons drawn. "She is a pain in the ass, you know. If I were you, I would have gotten rid of her a long time ago. She was - and is - a liability. Unfortunately, she was a necessary one, in order for us to get you. We will make bank with both of your captures, let alone the extra we get for your team."

He turned and left via the door the other two men had come out of.

One of the two men waved his gun at us. "Please follow him, gentlemen."

Baron glanced at me, grimacing. I shrugged and walked after the mercenary with Baron following. We both heard the door lock after we all had entered the hallway, following the lead man to the elevator, which was waiting and ready. Once we were all on board, the doors closed and the car slid down the shaft, heading for a lower floor.

My eyes traveled over the men, assessing them. The well-trained, and highly paid, mercenaries knew their stuff. I had worked with men like these. Unfortunately, these were now working for Edward. Which meant that if I had my way, they would all die.

The elevator stopped, and the doors opened silently. This hallway was like the one above. It was hard to see anything except closed doors. The man carrying Tessa walked down the hall, stopping in front of a random door and entering it. The men that were surrounding us passed that one and entered the next one down.

It was a lab, and I saw Holden on a table, hooked up to several pieces of equipment. My heart jumped. Then Holden turned her head and met my eyes.

Holden. I reached out to her. Her eyes went wide and then narrowed.

Shane, Edward is crazy. He thinks I am a hybrid lycanthrope - werewolf and human! He wants to breed me with another lycanthrope that he has in a cage...

I wasn't even sure if she knew she was talking to me via a mental bond, but I was glad that Edward could not hear what she said.

She glanced over to the wall where the cage was and gasped. I turned and looked. The mercenary who had led us here was placing Tessa into a glass cage next to the one holding a naked man crouching in a corner. Then the mercenary left, leaving her a prisoner.

"Who is that?" Holden croaked; her voice hoarse.

I tensed until Baron touched my arm. I forced myself to relax, but I wanted to go over to my mate.

Another man, one that I hadn't noticed before, moved. He chortled, watching us and glancing at the glass cages.

"Welcome to my lab. You must be Baron, the Alpha. See, Holden? The Alpha werewolf has come for you. I see he brought one of his wolves. I suspect it is one of his Betas. I am waiting to hear when my team has captured the others, which should be soon, but having an Alpha and Beta werewolf here in my lab right now is something I didn't think I would get without breeding them myself."

"What?" Holden looked back at me. I couldn't look at her, though. I didn't want to take my eyes off Edward, who was the biggest danger.

She snorted in frustration, though. "Those are not werewolves, you crazy ass! They are people that I know! Shane is one of my employers, in fact!"

"Oh, no. No, no, no. You have that wrong, sister-in-law. These men turn into wolves. These men are not human at all." Edward stalked closer, keeping Holden between him and us.

Tessa woke then, screaming. The noise only penetrated a little, but it was enough that we all turned our heads to look at the woman. She threw herself at the glass, pounding on it. The man next to her just crouched down smaller, trying to disappear. His eyes glinted, though, and he raised his nose a little to sniff in her direction.

Edward exhaled, watching her.

“Shut up, you stupid bitch.” The calm tone of his voice made my skin crawl. I didn’t like the woman, but I didn’t want to see what Edward would do to her either.

“That one, Holden. Wasn’t she with them?” Edward pointed at the woman, turning to look at her.

“Edward.” Her voice was soft, as if she was trying to placate him. “I have never seen her in my life. I have only been with Shane and Max. I have met Baron once, but no one else. The rest were just natural wolves. Because that is what I am - what I do. I am a wolf researcher. I was working with wolves.”

There was a sadness in her tone that pulled at my heart, even as I felt guilty for lying to her. Holden cared that Edward was bat-shit crazy. I huffed. She didn’t realize that even though we were all speaking English, everyone - except her - were communicating in an unfamiliar language. One where we understood the words, but she didn't.

"You have never seen her before?" Edward sounded confused.

Holden shook her head.

"But they are like Mercer, Holden. Like you. She can change into a wolf." Edward pointed at Tessa in the cage who had now sunk to the floor crying, finally realizing that Edward would not treat her like the princess she thought she was. "And him and him." He pointed at Baron and me, before walking closer to Holden and studying her. "And you." He added.

Holden shook her head. "I cannot change, Edward. I don't know what you saw in my DNA, but I am human. If I was a werewolf, or lycanthrope, wouldn't I have changed before this? I am almost thirty. I haven't changed. I won't ever change."

Edward's eyes took on a gleam. "Not unless you have a catalyst of some sort. Perhaps if I force you into heat. These male wolves would want you then. Perhaps they will force you to change for them." His voice was almost a mumble as he pulled out a syringe and plunged it into the line going into Holden's veins.

I took a step forward, my growl silent, but Baron touched my arm to hold me back. This was not the time to attack the man. He was too close to Holden. But I felt the need to protect my mate. This man was hurting her for a stupid reason. Holden was human. There had never been a human-lycanthrope hybrid.

I sent a pulse down the bond towards Shaz, acting as an inquiry. A few minutes passed and five pulses came back from him. Five minutes away. Another two came from Splinter and one from Erin. The team was almost in place. I just wasn't sure what the mercenaries' instructions were and if any of them or Edward would hurt Holden, but I needed to do something soon.

I shifted my body, trying to get into a position where it would be harder for someone to shoot me and hit something vital.

Holden twisted on the table and screamed, her voice sounding like a mix between human and wolf. I hesitated, my breath hitching. What had that mad man given her?

I sniffed, my nose catching her rising pheromones. Damn it! Was some of what Edward said true?

Was Holden a lycanthrope?

Mercer uncoiled from the corner of his cage, growling as he moved closer to the glass. He was sniffing the air, his nostrils flaring. It appeared he was trying to contain his shift, but wasn't successful as the hairs kept coming and receding on his arms and torso.

Even Baron was turning towards her, his face tilted up to catch her scent. Edward chortled, not noticing a ceiling tile move above him. Erin plummeted, bringing Edward down with her. Mark was right behind her, although he froze once he got to the floor.

Secure him. Work with Erin. I commanded, hoping that the male could resist Holden, given he was more interested in males. In fact, Mark turned and looked at Mercer, his grin wide while he put one foot on Edward's arm, holding it there.

Baron had turned back as soon as Erin had dropped, attacking the mercenary behind him. I moved towards Holden as an explosion rocked another lab door.

Splinter came in, his weapon pointed at the other mercenary. Both he, and Boomer behind him, groaned, almost losing their focus. Thank god we had trained for scenarios like this, where pheromones may be high and impacting the men on the mission. I knew that they could work through this. I was more worried about the others coming in. Shaz, Mac and Terry hadn't had this training and wouldn't be able to resist her right now.

Shaz! Wait a few minutes before entering the lab. They pumped Holden full of hormones and she is in heat! I started pulling the tubes and needles from her as she squirmed on the table.

The man's voice was just a growl coming down the Pack bonds. Damn it! Edward had installed a powerful ventilation system in this lab.

I looked around. There was a door on the far side, which I suspected was an office, but there might not be another way out of there. Not when there were male wolves in rut. I was sure that Edward had a bullet-hole escape route, but it worried me I might not find it before the wolves broke down the door.

There was only one thing to do. I snatched up Holden, threw her over my shoulder, and turned and ran for the door to the hallway. I danced around Mac and hit Shaz in the shoulder with my free hand, spinning the man around. Terry was standing just outside in the hallway, and he growled, his eyes on Holden's ass.

I growled louder, extending my power to those still around me. I heard yelps as some lesser wolves dropped to their knees, including Terry in front of me. I heard Baron's answering growl, him still in his human form, but close to turning.

"Get Edward!" I yelled over my shoulder at my Alpha while I ran for the stairs. I didn't want to get enclosed in the elevator with another one of my Pack and have to fight my way out. I hoped that Baron would take care of the real enemy, but I couldn't stay and ensure it. Safeguarding Holden was more important right now.

I reached the top of the stairs and extended my senses. There was someone scrabbling into the stairwell below me, but I couldn't hear or smell anyone on the other side of the door. I opened the stairwell door and then ducked, dodging the gun shot that then ricocheted down the stairs. I heard a yelp. I hoped that the bullet had only grazed whoever was behind me. If they were Pack.

Perfectly okay if it was a direct hit on a mercenary.

I stood, my gun in my hand, and shot once, twirling and shooting twice more. I hit both men that were guarding the door but didn't think any were kill shots. Lucky for me, they had unlocked the door to the lobby, so I ran, making for the outside door. I swerved, missing the shot that had come at me from the side. I had hoped that they wouldn't try to kill Holden, but the mercenaries didn't seem to pull their shots. A second bullet missed me by inches.

Bursting through the front door, I leaped to my left and ducked behind a large bush, panting. I felt a hand caress my ass, and I groaned softly.

"Holden! Please, not now."

"Shane!" Holden's voice was seductive. She reached for me with one hand while running the other down my back.

Nice she hadn't tried this earlier, but I didn't want to fight her off while dodging bullets.

Three men burst through the door, stopping just feet away from us, their heads swiveling. Not lycanthropes. Otherwise, they would have smelled her.

Quiet. I pushed the command down my mate

bond connection to Holden, hoping that she heard me. She stilled, so I took it as the gift it was. I lowered her to the ground, keeping a hand on her shoulder to hold her down.

Pulling out my gun, I realized I had one chance. There were three of them, and as soon as I shot the first, the other two could take me out.

Shit on a brick.

I checked the Pack bonds. Mac and Terry were running up the stairs, almost to the top. Both were in their wolf form and were hunting Holden. I could make use of that.

Mercenaries! I shouted at the two of them, down their personal connections. I sent a visual of the men. The wolves bounded up the last of the stairs and burst through the door into the lobby, heading for the three men.

Two of them turned to look at the attacking wolves, their eyes wide as they started shooting. I took aim on the third, an older man who ignored the commotion behind him.

I shot him, hitting his right shoulder, twirling the man around. The guy was a professional and shifted his gun to his left hand, shooting back.

The bullet grazed my cheek, leaving a trail of fire. I couldn't think of that, though, and shot the man again, as the two wolves exploded out the front door, attacking the other two mercenaries.

This time, I had gone with a head shot. The man fell to the ground, surprise covering his face. I picked up Holden, realizing I was almost out of time, and threw her again over my shoulder, running straight for Baron's truck. I hoped that it would take time for Mac and Terry to take down the two mercenaries. Then they would not try to get into Holden's pants. Fucking aphrodisiac!

I opened the passenger side door, shoving her in.

Worry filled me. She was quiet because she was unconscious. I just hoped no one had shot her. I couldn't check, though, so I pulled the seat belt over her, clicking it shut, and closed the door.

Mac must have already dispatched his target since he was charging towards me. I leaped up onto the hood of the truck and slid over it, coming down on the driver's side. Getting in, I had just slammed the door shut when Mac hit the side of the truck with a thunk.

"Keys. Keys." Mumbling, I reached over and opened the glove compartment. There they were.

Another thump sounded and I looked up. Terry was on the hood, staring down at me, his teeth bared. I shoved the keys into the ignition and started the truck up, slamming it into reverse. I heard a yelp, but Terry was still somehow hanging onto the hood, so it had to have been Mac.

I hoped that Baron wouldn't be mad about the claw marks on his truck. Putting it into drive, I started forward before swerving. Terry's claws scratched the hood's paint as he slid off it, falling to the road. He yipped in pain.

Wolves poured out of the building, with Baron in their midst, still in his human shape standing among them.

Watching in my rear-view mirror as I peeled down the street, I saw Baron salute me and then put his hands on his hips. I could feel the Alpha pull the Pack back to him, struggling to get his wolves back under control now that Holden and her pheromones were leaving the vicinity. I hoped that they also had secured Edward, but I couldn't worry about that. Holden came first.

I drove, taking turns and speeding through towns, hoping there was no one following us. I was glad I had gotten Holden out of there. Even if whatever

Edward had done to her had exhausted her. As dusk fell, I circled around and headed into the woods not too far from the compound. I entered them from the east, finding the right gravel road. I traveled it for about twenty minutes before pulling up beside a lone cabin.

Stopping, I inhaled. Whatever had been in that syringe Edward had given her was wearing off. Glancing over, I noticed her breathing was even and soft. I sighed, wiping sweat from my face. Grimacing, I noticed I was still bleeding from the facial graze. I wiped my bloody hand on my pants and then got out, suddenly light-headed.

Fuck! I only knew of the one bullet grazing my cheek, but I wasn't sure if someone had hit me somewhere else. It didn't matter. I had to get Holden inside. Leaning against the car, I staggered to the passenger side door and opened it. I would make it inside. I had to.

Unbuckling her seat belt, I then pulled her into my embrace. She felt heavy to me. I walked towards the cabin, but every step felt like it was harder than the one before. I stumbled up the steps and put a palm against a panel next to the door.

I was glad I had installed the Biometric Lock the

last time I had gotten hurt. It's a real bitch to search for the damn key with a severe injury. I keyed this lock to let me in, either in wolf or human form. The only other person who had access was Max, since when I came here, I needed a doctor. In fact, Max would get a text that the lock had opened as soon as I unlocked it. Which meant he would come here and save my ass. I wasn't sure where my injury was, but I was losing a lot of blood.

Darn silver bullets.

I heard the click as the lock disengaged and shoved the door open. I made it to the couch, laying Holden down on it before I collapsed to the floor.

Chapter 19

Shane

“Is he okay?” I heard Holden’s voice whisper nearby and realized that she was already up and about.

“I think so. I need him awake for his treatment. I cannot determine how bad things are when he is unconscious.”

Max was being vague, not knowing if Holden knew we were lycanthropes. I wasn’t even sure if she knew I was one, even though she now knew lycanthropes existed. Time to get this out in the open.

I blinked open my eyes, groaning at the bright light shining in them. Fuck. I squeezed them closed.

"Damn it, Shane." Max swore at me. I watched the redness from behind my eyelids fade and then the doctor tapped my arm. "I don't have the damn light in your eyes now, and Holden has dimmed the overheads. Open your eyes."

I did, squinting at the man in front of me. Max looked worried, even though he was trying to hide it from the woman beside him. I glanced over to her and realized that the doctor wasn't fooling her.

"I am sorry, Shane, but you need to shift." His voice low, Max touched my chest. "Someone got you in the chest, breaking a rib and leaving a silver bullet in there. I have removed the bullet, but the bleeding isn't stopping. I think if you shift, you will heal."

I opened my eyes wide, my eyes flicking to Holden. She stood there, her arms around herself as if she was holding herself together.

"Can I...?" My voice gave out, and I had to start again. "I need a moment with Holden, Max."

Max nodded, standing up. "I am sorry." I knew he was sorrier about how I had to tell Holden than about me having to shift.

The doctor slipped out of the room. A few moments later, I heard the external door open and then close.

Holden stayed where she was, staring at me. I sighed.

"Holden." I put out a hand. She moved to my side, helping me to sit up.

"You're a lycanthrope, aren't you, Shane? A werewolf?" Her voice was low and emotionless.

I nodded. "I am. Well, we don't use the term werewolf. I was born this way. Born into a Pack. Most everyone around here has been. Maggie? She is a very submissive wolf in Baron's Pack. Lexi, Soren, and Betta? They are my brother's pups. Someone killed their parents - my brother and his mate - and stole their pups. By Edward, Holden. Lexi confirmed that he is the bad man she mumbles about, scared out of her mind."

She shifted back to her human form, her arms back around her waist. "Max? Is he even a doctor?"

I chuckled. "Yes, he is. Lycanthropes can be doctors. Lycanthropy isn't a virus. It is not contagious. He cannot pass Lycanthropy onto anyone he treats. Only a few rare cases of bitten wolves exist. It is hard to transfer the necessary… I don't know, magic perhaps… to a human so they can shift. If they survive the first transformation, we then invite them to enter a Pack." I shrugged.

"What about me?"

"What?" I stared at her, not understanding.

She grimaced, wrinkling her nose in a way that I thought was adorable.

"Edward mentioned that I was a hybrid. Having both human and lycanthrope genes." She paused and then added. "No wolf bit me, Shane. I was born, but my father died when I was seven. I don't remember him going furry, but I remember how warm he was."

Her voice took on a sing-song aspect as she continued, lost in her memories. "He was the one that gave me my love of wolves. He would tell me so many stories, show me wolf tracks, help me learn about pups. I would sit on his lap at night, snuggled up against his very warm chest while he talked with me and my mother, falling asleep to his warmth."

Ah, that made more sense. Her father was the lycanthrope. He had been preparing his daughter for life as a wolf if she ever shifted. But she hasn't. At least, not yet.

If she had human genes, her mother must have been human, but special. Hybrids didn't happen. Humans and Lycanthropes typically could not breed - they didn't have either human babies or wolf pups. Which explained why Holden and Thomas never had kids.

Her gaze sharpened on me. "Why would Edward think I could breed with wolves.... lycanthropes? Thomas and I couldn't have children. Why would he think Mercer and I could have them?"

Anger flashed through me at the wolf's name before I wrestled it into the background. The thought of her with any other wolf made me want to claim her right here and now.

Getting my emotions under control, I shrugged. "I am not sure. I know little at all about hybrids. Perhaps we can ask Max. I don't know if he knows anything, but we can always ask him."

She nodded and then released her arms; her face looking concerned. She knelt and looked at my chest. "You are still bleeding, Shane. Let me get

Max." She stood and started for the door.

"I need to shift, Holden. I will be a wolf, but I will also still be me. Here, inside." I tapped on my chest with a finger. I wasn't sure if she had heard me.

I sighed. I swung my feet over the side of the bed and groaned. Yea. Max had gotten rid of my jeans and put me into shorts. I wasn't sure I could stand, so I just pushed my shorts down, pooling at my feet, leaning forward and calling my wolf to the fore.

Changing hurt. I suspected it was because there was so much silver still in my bloodstream. Still, this pain was more than usual.

I was panting on the floor when Max returned, Holden right behind him. The doctor knelt and put his hand in my fur, digging deep into my neck muscles to relax the tension he could feel from me through the Pack connection. He sighed, running a hand down my wolf's side to check the wounds. I flinched a time or two when his hand touched sensitive parts.

"How is he?" Holden asked. Max looked up at her. "Sore, but the bleeding has stopped. He still has two broken ribs, so I want him to shift a few more times, except I don't think he can do that yet. Come and sit by his head, Holden, while I get him some food and water."

Holden sat by my head, cross-legged. I whined and shifted around so that my immense head was in her lap, licking her leg.

Max chuckled, shook his head, and rose, leaving the room to go into the kitchen.

"Shane?"

Holden. I answered, using my mate bond to talk with her. Exhaustion colored my tone.

She almost jumped up, startled. "I was talking with you!" Her hand landed on my neck, her fingers clinching the thick fur that was there.

I sighed, snuggling my head in more. *Yes*.

Holden massaged my neck muscles, and I melted. It felt so good to my wolf to have her touch me, to know about me. She wasn't running, which made my wolf ecstatic. And while her pheromones were less, I could smell that she would enter a true heat soon, not the artificial one that Edward had tried to induce.

Max entered with two bowls, one filled with meat

and the other with water.

"Shane, I need you to be an obedient patient for us, please. I mixed the meat with an antibiotic. I know you will taste it but eat, anyway. For Holden."

He put the bowls down near my head. Holden picked up a chunk and offered it to me. I sniffed and then groaned, hiding my head in her lap.

"Come on, Shane, you need this medicine." Holden pulled on my fur, lifting my head. She held the meat in front of me, the look on her face determined. "Eat this."

Neither I nor my wolf could resist the dominant tone she had used. In fact, my wolf wanted to whine and go belly up. I huffed at the silly beast, before taking the meat and chewing. I swallowed the mouthful with a wolf grimace.

Max laughed. "Good luck getting enough of that in his stomach, Holden. He needs it, but he will fight you all the way. Once he finishes, though, we should have him shift back to human and I will look him over. I suspect I will have to have him cycle between wolf and human a few times before he gets to the stage I want him at."

I growled at the doctor. Holden smacked my muzzle, startling both Max and me.

"Stop that." Her voice was absentminded, her expression thoughtful.

My wolf stared up at her, my eyes wide.

Max barked out a laugh. "Shane, you have met your match! Holden, please make him your mate and put the rest of us out of misery from having to deal with this bullheaded male."

He continued out into the living room, his chuckles coming back in intervals.

Holden held up another piece of the abhorrent meat, her eyes expectant. I grimaced. Then I ate the meat my mate provided.

Holden

"Enough."

Even in his human form, he growled the word out.

"I think he has lost all patience for this." I studied the man lying on the floor, his face resolute. I couldn't help admiring his body, given he was naked in front of me. Shane had a gorgeous body, firm with fluid muscles that moved under smooth tan skin. "Perhaps we should stop."

I shook my head, fanning myself from the sudden heat I felt, and headed to the couch. Max finished checking Shane's ribs, his naked front turned away from me, thank god. After a few stressful moments, the doctor sat back on his heels.

"Good enough. Go get dressed, Shane. We can do the rest with you as a human. It will be nice to hear more than growls and whimpers out of you."

"Asshole." Shane stood, grabbing a nearby blanket to wrap around himself, before shuffling off into the bedroom, closing the door without it making a sound.

Max sighed and joined me. "And that, dear Holden, was Shane's method of slamming a door and saying 'Fuck you'."

I giggled, resting my head against the back of the couch. "Wow. If it wasn't for my exhaustion, I think I would be excited about this new field of study. Lycanthropes. Who would have figured?"

Max gave me a strange glance, but before he could say anything, the front door of the cabin flew open, banging against the wall.

Three little kids, around the age of six, charged in. A woman who looked to be in her early twenties followed them. The kids flung themselves at me, holding onto me tight. I turned wide, confused eyes towards the doctor.

"Who...?"

Max laughed, knowing I hadn't a clue who these children were and why they were enthusiastically hugging me. He pulled a dark-haired little girl off of me, setting her in his lap. The girl squirmed, but he held her tight.

"Betta, please sit still. Lexi and Soren, we just introduced Holden to lycanthropes, so she doesn't know you are the wolf pups she has been caring for."

The little boy and girl froze, their eyes wide. They lifted their heads to stare at me. I stared back at them, taking in the doctor's words.

"Lexi? This is Lexi?" I touched the little girl's cheek, taking in her red-hair and emerald green eyes. Those eyes.... Yes, those were Lexi's eyes. I shifted my gaze to the little boy. "Soren?" He was a looker, his hair a mixture of red and dark brown, his eyes gray. His solemn stare gave me the feeling that he had the weight of the world on his shoulders.

I then turned my head towards the dark brown-haired little girl, with wide, worried blue eyes. "Betta." The word was a whisper. I put out my arm and Max released the girl as she flew into my grasp.

I held the three children tight. Tears flowed down my face as I mumbled words of love and astonishment at them. I only had two arms, but I filled them with the three small children and they were not complaining about the lack of room on my lap.

Shane came out of the bedroom, pulling a shirt over his low-lying jeans. I figured he had heard the door.

I looked up at him, my watery grin ecstatic.

"My puppies!"

I didn't care if they were wolves or children. I loved them as they were.

Shane exhaled in relief, moving to sit on the arm of the couch.

Lexi patted my face in her small hands. She wiggled around so she could meet my eyes. "Mama Holden. We wanted to change and show you, but we couldn't. We weren't sure you would love us because we had wolves. Would the Bad Man find us? But he came anyway and took you. We are so glad that Uncle Shane got you back. We will help him keep the Bad Man away from you."

Soren, his face so serious, nodded in agreement.

Betta just reached up and kissed my cheek. I laughed and then cried, holding the pups tighter.

Shane glanced at the young woman standing near the door. "Maggie, please come over here and sit. Holden will want to meet you."

I looked up, my face startled. "Maggie? This is Maggie?" Bemused, I looked between Shane and the young woman.

Shane nodded. "Yes, this is Maggie. You knew her as the wolf who played with the pups."

Betta spoke up. "Maggie is nice. I like her. We like her. She is family, Uncle Shane. Pack."

Shane smiled, as if he knew what Betta was saying. "Yes, Betta, she is Pack."

The little girl smiled back at her uncle before snuggling back in against me and her siblings.

Maggie smiled. "I have been watching them for you, Holden. They are good pups. So easy to love. I would love to continue helping you with them if you will have me."

Her voice was soft and melodic, a slight accent sounding every so often, even though I wasn't sure what it was.

I studied the woman, wondering what…

"Omega! You are an Omega. You are not a submissive wolf at all! Omegas help to bind a Pack together." I somehow bounced on the couch, still holding the pups. "I cannot believe that your Pack has an Omega, Shane! I have heard about these in natural wolf Packs, but they are so rare!"

The other three adults stared at me. Max was the first to recover, shaking his head. "Of course! I should have guessed, given how much easier it has been to treat wolves with her around." He grimaced.

Shane stared at him. "What?"

Max looked at the woman in question. "Maggie,

you are not the bottom of the Pack. You are one of the most important. You help keep a Pack healthy, both physically and mentally. Baron will want to keep you once he finds out, though, because Omegas are so rare. Shane may have a fight on his hands."

Soren peeked at Maggie, sliding off my lap and scampering over to the woman. "No, Maggie. You are ours. You are not part of that Pack, but ours. Please don't go."

The look of astonishment left the other woman's eyes. She pulled Soren onto her lap and he hugged her, his nose tucked into her neck. "I will stay with you if I can, Soren."

Shane snorted. I figured that Baron would not win this fight. Maggie was part of Shane's Pack. Sadness filled me. I wished I could be a part of his Pack, like Lexi had said. Unfortunately, I was human.

Shane looked down at me. I hugged the two little girls, so alike and yet so different. Lexi had her arms tight around one of mine, her body curled up on most of my lap, her head lying against my chest.

"It looks like you have two sleepy pups there,

Holden." His voice was deep, filled with emotion.

I looked down and smiled. "Lexi is out, and Betta looks like she will be soon."

Shane gave Max a look, and he threw his hands up in the air. "All right!"

Confusion crossed my face as Max stood and picked up Betta, nodding at Maggie and moving to the door. "We are taking the pups back to the compound. You two need to clear up a few things. You do not need to involve the pups in that."

Maggie lifted Soren, who yawned, and joined the doctor at the door.

Shane stood and put out his arms. "I'll take Lexi, Holden."

I tightened my grip on the little girl. "Shane!" My wail was soft, since I didn't want to wake Lexi.

Shane bent down and kissed me on the lips. I turned my face up to him, wanting more, but he pulled back. "I want that too, but first, let's get the pups settled. And kick Maggie and Max out. They will take good care of them, Holden, while we talk."

I knew what he was implying, so I let Lexi go, my hands reluctant as they trailed a caress along the little girl's arms. Shane picked her up and followed Maggie and Max.

Chapter 20

Shane

I closed the door, listening to the sound of the truck leaving behind me, and watched Holden.

Holden shifted on the couch. She noticed my solemn face. I rubbed my eyes, not sure if I wanted to have this conversation but knowing we had to have it.

"What is it?"

I blew out a puff of air and rubbed my face. Moving towards her, I opted to take the chair across from her. I slumped, my eyes closed.

"Edward got away." My words were quiet, except they seemed to boom out into the room.

She stiffened, her eyes searching my face. "He....

got away?" She didn't understand. I don't think she wanted to understand.

I nodded and turned my head to look at her. "Somehow, in all the confusion, he slipped away. Baron said he was unconscious when he had turned to get Tessa out of the cage, but Edward had disappeared when he returned for him minutes later. We thought we had all the mercenaries, but there may have been one or two hidden that helped him escape."

She sat there, shaking. She pulled a blanket around her, bundling herself up before pulling up her feet so she could rest her chin on her knees and hide everything up to her head.

"He is dangerous, Shane."

"I know."

"And he will come after me again. He thinks I am this hybrid human-lycanthrope being. He doesn't understand that I am not a wolf, that I cannot shift."

I wanted to reach out and hold her, but I suspected she wouldn't welcome me right then. "Yet you can talk via the Pack bonds. You smell just like a wolf to us - enough that you drove the

Pack males wild." I hesitated, and then continued even softer, deciding to lay all my cards on the table. "And my wolf says you are my mate. He has always wanted you. I have always agreed with him — I want you. Something is different about you — more than any other human woman I have met."

We sat there; the room growing darker as night fell outside. Holden just stared at the floor while I watched her. I couldn't take the silence any longer and I stood, moving towards the kitchen. I opened the refrigerator and took out a casserole dish.

"Lasagna okay?" I asked over a shoulder, diving back inside to pull out a salad. Not waiting for her answer, I placed both on the counter and turned the dial on the stove to preheat it. Turning back around, I leaned against the counter to wait for it to get warm.

Holden stared out into the room, her voice almost a murmur to herself. "My father always called me his pup. My mother would call me her miracle child. I never thought those endearments would be hints I was different."

"What else did they say that seemed a little odd?"

Holden snorted. "I was a child, Shane. Much of what they said seemed odd. I remember them being so in love, and yet they never let me feel like a third wheel. They would finish each other's sentences and seemed to communicate without words." A small smile touched her lips. "They were always touching each other, little touches that showed how much they were in love."

I nodded. Mate bond.

Her eyes widened. "My parents bonded, didn't they? They could talk in their heads like we do?"

I smiled, nodding. My mate was learning what it meant to be a lycanthrope. Her entire past was being rewritten as she learned about my world. I wished that Edward and his crazy issues hadn't forced it on her like this. And yet, I wasn't sure if there was a good way to get to this point.

The oven beeped, and I turned to place the dish in it, setting the timer for twenty minutes. I stared at the salad bowl, realizing that I had taken it out too early. I returned it to the fridge, pulling out a beer instead.

"Beer? Wine?" I held the fridge door open, looking towards Holden.

“Hot tea on the list?”

I nodded, shutting the door before filling the kettle and plugging it in to heat. I pulled out a tea bag and a mug from the cabinet.

This felt homey, and yet tension filled the room.

I turned and looked at her, deciding to just come clean.

“I am a wolf, Holden.”

She looked at me, wary. “I know.”

“My wolf is certain that you are our mate. He feels that you could shift if you wanted to. I think that is what Edward was trying to force. You to shift. To activate the lycanthrope part of you.”

She stared back at me. “That is what I don’t understand, Shane. Lycanthropes, by definition, are both human and wolf. What makes me different? Why did he call me a hybrid, as if I was a different breed?”

Shit. She was right. I wasn’t sure what the difference was, just that Holden felt different to me from other lycanthropes.

Max. I searched for the doctor, finding him talking with Maggie and Sarah, his wife, at the compound.

I wondered when you would ask. The reply was instantaneous.

You should have just said something. So what makes Holden different? What makes a hybrid different?

I could hear the doctor's sigh across the bond. *There's not much difference that we know. But there haven't been that many hybrids and most of them have been male - and sterile. Holden not only isn't male but also can breed, given the pheromones she was giving off earlier. Hybrid females should have an easier time carrying our young, since they won't have the same urge to shift, if they can even shift at all. That is one of the larger differences I know about. We - lycanthropes - cannot breed with humans. We might breed with a hybrid, even if they cannot shift. They share our DNA, which would make it easier for them to have pups.*

I interjected. *So, she may not shift*?

What Holden is, Shane, is unknown. One male could shift, but it was slow and painful. So much so he didn't do it, outside of twice, the first time because something had frightened him into it.

Another got stuck between wolf and human, and they executed him. I am not sure if any of the others even tried.

Do you know if any of them had mates? I wondered if mate bonding would make a difference.

That caused Max to pause. I could imagine the wheels turning, the doctor accessing the vast information in his brain.

Good point. The response came slower. *I don't think any of them were. The researchers isolated them after they found the hybrids, so I would have to presume that, no, they didn't have mates*. He paused again. *Are you going to bond with Holden? Are you going to mate bond with her*?

I think I already have. With that, I closed the communication pathway, blocking the doctor. I knew that Max might otherwise have checked in to see how things were going if I left it open. And this, whatever it was between Holden and me, was only between the two of us.

Looking up, I saw that Holden was waiting, her impatience showing. Damn, that was rude of me.

"Sorry." I raised my eyebrows in placation,

twisting my mouth. "I was, well.... Talking with Max. I wasn't sure of the answer to your question and wanted to ask him."

"And?" I could see she was resisting jiggling her leg.

"And a hybrid is different because it is possible you may not shift, even though you have some DNA of a lycanthrope. Most of the other hybrids had been male and sterile. First, you are not male. And we doubt you are sterile. The result? We are not sure what you can do."

"Sterile?" There was a touch of horror in her tone. I remembered that Holden had tried to have a child before, with Thomas. I sought to ease her mind, rushing over and taking her hand.

"Holden, Edward did one thing right. He gave you something that proved you are fertile and that you can attract other lycanthropes. Even though, I could have told you that, years ago. My wolf stood up inside me and wanted to make you ours back then. He thought you were our mate, but the human me needed to wait, to make sure. And then the war came, the explosion happened, and you got married because you thought I was dead."

My thumb rubbed a soft circle on her palm as I

continued.

“There are no studies that explain you. We have found no one like you, that we know of. Except, perhaps, one of your parents. Given what you said about your father, the hybrid would have been your mother. Your parents conceived you. And you…”

I lifted her hand and placed a gentle kiss on her palm.

“You might have pups. You might not. But to tell you the truth, I don’t care. I have my nieces and my nephew. I want you, not your ability to breed. If we have pups, great. But I want you, Holden. I want to mate with you.”

Her eyes shone with tears, but her voice didn’t shake.

“How does one mate?”

I stood, rushing back into the kitchen to turn the oven down to warm and unplugging the kettle, before returning to her. Pulling her hand towards me, I lifted her so she stood up against my body. We moved through the living room and entered the bedroom, standing beside the bed. Dropping her hand, I cradled her face in my hands and stared down at her.

"It entails making love with you, Holden. I have been looking forward to this moment for so very long. It means giving you everything that I am - the wolf, the man, the Beta and the Alpha parts of me. There is a lot of pleasure and a little of pain, because every relationship has these facets. But then the pleasure comes back tenfold."

She looked up at me, her eyes wide. I lowered my head slowly, holding her face. I wanted to give her time to move, to put a stop to this if she wanted to. But if she didn't, I would make her mine.

Mine! My wolf howled inside my head.

Yours. A soft voice whispered in response.

And then my lips touched hers.

Holden

Having Shane kiss me was like nothing I have ever experienced. Thomas was a good kisser, except there had been something missing. Something I never knew I searched for. I thought the thing missing was my fault. But with Shane, I found that it wasn't me; it had been us. What had been missing from my life was Shane.

Home.

He tasted like home. He felt like home as I slid my hands around him, sliding them under his T-shirt and up his back, feeling the hard muscles there.

It didn't matter that this man was not human. That he turned into a big, bad, furry wolf. All that mattered is that this was my friend, someone I could talk to, the one I had thought I had lost because of a stupid war.

I wanted to climb up him and wrap my limbs around him, holding him to me forever so he could never leave me again.

His lips left mine and moved down my neck, leaving a trail of kisses, before stopping at my shoulder. He took in a breath, his large body shuddering, before he returned to my mouth, his lips moving over my own. I opened my mouth, and he grabbed my bottom lip with his teeth before releasing it. One large hand slipped down to my ass, massaging the muscle there. My stomach quivered in anticipation.

I grew desperate to feel him, all of him. Pulling his shirt up, I grunted. He laughed, raising his arms up so I could push it up as high as I could. Shane was a large man and I couldn't get it over his head. He laughed again and helped me, throwing the shirt into a corner before wrapping me in his arms again.

His skin smelled wonderful - warm and musky, like pine trees and fur. I rubbed my cheek on his chest, the light hairs tickling my chin. I heard his heart speed up, a growl building inside his chest. I smiled, sticking out my tongue to lick at a nipple.

Shane shivered and then groaned. One big hand came up to hold my head against him. I smiled again, knowing what he wanted. I latched onto his nipple and sucked it in, my teeth holding the small bud between them before releasing it to suck on it once again.

He pulled on my hair, tilting my head back until his nipple came out of my mouth with a slight pop. He took my mouth, as if he was searching for something that he needed to find. I opened to him, my fingers digging into his back muscles. His kiss softened and his hands moved to remove my shirt before his mouth moved down to lick that area where my neck met my shoulder.

Now it was my turn to shudder.

He looked up at me, and his smile was seductive.

“Mine.”

The word hung in the air as we delved into each other, learning what it meant to be soul-bound. Mated.

Chapter 21

Holden

I stretched, feeling deliciously sore in all the right places. Muscles that hadn't had a workout in a while complained as I moved. I enjoyed making love with Thomas, but making love to Shane had broken me apart and put me back together again as a new person.

Flinging my arms wide, I smiled and then frowned. I turned my head, noticing the indentation in the pillow next to me. Felt the slight coolness of the sheets.

Where had he gone?

I sat up and reached out with my mind. He was in the living room. Huh, this bond stuff made finding him easy. Smiling, I swung my legs out of bed and stood, wincing when I rolled my shoulders. Walking into the bathroom, I looked at my left shoulder.

A bite mark. The mating bite mark.

I studied it, noticing the canine teeth that no human would have. I wondered if it would heal or if it would stay red, just like this. Something inside me wanted it to stay. I wanted to show everyone, in particular, any bitch who might have thoughts about encroaching upon my beautiful man.

I shook my head, smiling. This was so not me. I wondered if this was part of my lycanthrope DNA bubbling up. I would have to ask Max.

I took a quick shower and dressed, walking out into the living room barefooted, braiding my wet hair. Shane was there, as was Max. Baron and a familiar-looking woman stood next to the doctor.

"Holden." Shane's voice caressed my ears, the echo of love coming through his bond with me.

I sauntered up to him, tying off my braid. He put an arm around me, pulling me in tight. I tilted my head back to meet his kiss, my heart thrilling. Shane didn't just give me a quick peck, though.

He kissed me passionately, leaving me panting.

As I turned to look at our guests, my cheeks pink with embarrassment, I caught Max's eye-roll. He followed it with a smile of delight.

"Holden, I know you've met the Alpha, Baron, before. This here is his mate, Miranda. Miranda is Tessa's sister. Tessa was the wolf in the cage next to Mercer's."

I turned and studied the pair. Baron was smiling at me, but his mate's smile was a little more strained.

"I see congratulations are in store, Shane." The Alpha chuckled, delight filling his voice.

I put a hand over the mark, my face turning a bright red. Shane just laughed, pulling me in tighter.

"Thank you. Holden is the mate I have always wanted." He smiled down at me, his love clear. My embarrassment disappeared in that moment.

I smiled up at him and then watched the other woman. Miranda didn't look happy, but I couldn't figure out why. She already had a mate. Could lycanthropes desire someone who wasn't their own mate? That was not a typical wolf feature.

Max, ever observant, sighed. "Sorry, Holden. Miranda's sister - Tessa - had been the wolf that had jumped the fence to attack the pups. She also helped Edward with his plan to capture you."

Ah! The woman in the cage!

"But he turned on her, didn't he? He caged her. What happened to her? Come to think about it, what happened to Mercer as well?" Fellow victims of Edward should unite... well, at least talk together.

Baron fidgeted, which I thought was unusual for the Alpha wolf to do. Shane turned away, as if he didn't notice, and led us towards the sitting area, tucking me into the corner of a couch, before sitting right next to me. I glanced at him curiously, wondering why he was protecting me from his friends like this.

Max laughed. "Holden, your face!" He laughed even harder, while everyone turned to look at me. I went bright red once again and stared at the floor.

"I don't know what is so funny." The sullen words slipped out.

Max gasped out a few more laughs before wiping

his eyes. “Shane will protect you from everyone, friend or foe. He is very territorial. Mated males are.”

Baron chuckled, sitting in a chair and pulling Miranda down on his lap. “He is an Alpha, in his own right. I suspect he will want to start his own Pack, now that he has you. He always could.”

Miranda gasped. “Shane is an Alpha? Why would he be…”

Baron looked up at his mate, his hand brushing her cheek.

“Why would he be my Beta, my love? Because of the war. It broke him, even though he could have taken over the Pack then. He has been acting as Alpha, even more so since Holden has come back into his life.” He shrugged and then looked towards Shane. “Don’t think I didn’t notice you can command most of the Pack. That you were working the Pack communication bonds during this last mission, since you would use any resource to rescue Holden.”

Shane rubbed his mouth, his expression sheepish. “I didn’t want to undermine your authority, Baron, but I have more strategic experience than you. Everyone responded without even thinking about it, so I took advantage. I'm sorry."

Baron chuckled. "Yet you are not. Because by doing so, you now have Holden, not only next to your side, but bonded to you."

Shane just shrugged, a gleam in his eyes.

Max sighed, turning to me.

"To get back to the matter at hand, we released Mercer. He was a lone wolf before and wants to be again. What that means is that he doesn't want to have allegiance to any Pack. Tessa escaped in the confusion, as did Edward, but we don't think they are together." The doctor glanced at Miranda before looking back. "I suspect that Tessa is somewhere nearby, licking her wounds. She is a spoiled wolf, not understanding that she just can't get everything she wants with a flick of her fingers."

A soft whine filled the air.

Everyone turned to Miranda, who was looking down at her hands clasped in her lap.

"I am so sorry. I felt so bad when our parents died that I tried to make life easier for her. I guess I didn't help her understand how things worked."

"You think?" Baron's voice was wry.

Miranda deflated. "Our parents weren't part of a Pack, Baron. They were...... a pair of lone wolves that had gotten together to have pups. Tessa and me. We all kept to ourselves and they spoiled us rotten. When I had met and mated with you, my parents had been so angry with me. They had tried to stop all of my communication with my sister, but we somehow got notes to one another. When Tessa had shown up, telling me that our parents had died, I knew I had to take care of her. I had left her with them, and then she had no one else to turn to."

Baron shook his head, slow at first and then with a little more emphasis as she finished.

"She lied to you, Mira. She has always bent the truth to her own advantage. For one, your parents are still alive, living in the same cabin you grew up in. Tessa just left and followed you, afraid you were getting something she didn't have. When she found us mated, with me being an Alpha of a large Pack, she tried to seduce me, not realizing what a mate bond was and that I couldn't look at anyone but you. That is when I had her investigated. And found out she had lied to you about your parents."

Miranda's eyes widened, her gaze intent on her mate. "You never told me."

"No, I couldn't. I tried, many times, but somehow I knew it would have destroyed something inside of you and I couldn't be the one to hurt you." He frowned. "Shane told me I needed to tell you, that this would turn out bad otherwise, and it did. But I had always hoped that Tessa would just fess up. She just doesn't know how to be a part of a Pack. She understands nothing about being a lycanthrope, even if she has always been one of us. Your parents did her no service. I don't know how you accepted the concept of Pack and all that it means, but she just hasn't been able to adjust."

Max interrupted. "I suspect that a lot of it is the mate bond you have with Miranda. Information flows through it you don't even realize you are getting. Miranda learned a lot from you, but remember when she first arrived, she had made some large snafus."

Baron nodded; his face pensive. "You are right. No one wanted to mate with Tessa, even if she is a fine-looking wolf. She is, by nature, self-centered and mean, while you have a good, sweet soul."

Tears filled Miranda's eyes. "I am sorry that she caused so much disruption to the Pack."

Baron lifted her chin with one large hand. "No matter, love. We were dealing with it. Until now. Now she has gone too far and, I don't want to keep her in the Pack. At the very least, though, the Pack demands punishment."

Max looked at us all. "Or we could send her off with Mercer. He can't stand being in a Pack, at this point. Add to that, Edward isolated him for a very long time. He would chafe at Pack bonds. He is, though, interested in Tessa, since she is having trouble being in a Pack. He told me so when I was checking him over. He is strong enough to handle her, I think. I say, let her go off with him. He can always return with her later or take her back to her parents if things don't work out."

Shane nodded. "That would be a suitable solution, at least in the interim. I just think we need to make sure he knows who she is."

"He knows." Max's tone showed his determination. "I made sure he knew what he was signing up for. He seemed...... eager to take on such a task. I think being out of the military is boring for him."

"Huh." Baron's thoughtful tone rumbled. "Well, I approve. Miranda, tell Max where Tessa is, since I know you hid her to keep her away from us."

Miranda blushed, even though there was no reproach in her mate's voice. "She is at the North cabin."

Max took out his phone and sent the information to someone. I suspected Mercer was the one getting this information.

Baron turned to Shane and smiled. "Well, now that we took care of Mercer and Tessa, let's talk about you. Are you leaving to start your own Pack? And how many of mine are you taking with you?"

Shane chuckled, rubbing one of his hands over my knee.

"Are you pushing me out, Baron?"

Baron gave him a look. "Seriously, Shane. You should have left ages ago. You are an Alpha and have only remained with my Pack because of some convoluted sense of loyalty to me. So yes, if I must, I am kicking you out. I also realized a while back that I would have to give up some of my Pack, since they were your people. Miranda and I will move up north, leaving this southern area for you, since this is where Holden is most comfortable."

"Me?" That came out as a squeak.

Baron turned his dark eyes to me. "Yes, you, Holden. You are going through so many changes and new experiences right now. Learning you have lycanthrope DNA. Heck, learning lycanthropes even exist. Then you mated with an Alpha wolf who will start his own Pack. That means not only learning what it means to be a wolf but also what it means to be the Pack's Alpha female."

"I can help with that," Miranda interjected.

Baron glanced between the two women, noticing the discomfort I had around his mate. Ignoring that, he continued. "You also haven't shifted. We don't know if you even can. That may or may not cause issues with your Pack." He ignored the soft growl that came from Shane at that statement. "Having to leave a familiar place to start up somewhere new would be a lot for anyone to handle. I suspect you can do your research work from here, even though, that may be a bit weird."

I frowned at Baron, thinking. What was so weird about my job? A wolf biologist? Oh!

I started chuckling and soon was laughing so hard tears came out of my eyes. Baron grinned at me. It took a few more minutes before the rest caught on and started laughing with us.

"I guess I will have a definite advantage on my colleagues. Then again, I will have to pick what to research and write about. I don't think the general population is ready to learn about lycanthropes." I exhaled, wiping away the stray tears that had appeared when I had laughed. "In fact, it may just be easier to change to another species to study or some other research topic. With the fact I was on sabbatical, this may be the best time."

Shane pulled me in, offering me comfort both with his closeness and through our bond. I smiled up at him, my smile tinged with sadness.

He kissed the top of my head and then turned back to Baron.

"To answer your question, Lexi, Soren, and Betta are definite. Maggie wants to come, so that means Boomer will follow along since he is interested in our Omega. Splinter will follow since he has followed Boomer for years now. If you can give up Shaz, I wouldn't mind him in my group."

Baron slapped his hand down on the sides of the chair he was in. "Omega?"

Shane grinned at him. "Omega. Holden figured it out. You snooze, you lose, old wolf."

Baron snorted. "Huh."

"I would also like to go with Shane." Max spoke up. "I would love to work with Holden on some of her research, and we work well together." He paused and then blurted out. "Also, Sarah is pregnant again. I want to keep her around Maggie and Holden as much as possible to ensure that the pup survives the pregnancy this time. She has always had a hard time not shifting for so long."

I leaned forward. "What can I do to help her, Max? I know nothing about lycanthropes or shifting. Or birthing pups either."

"You don't shift. Even if you learn to, you will have a greater control over shifting. That control, if it travels via Pack bonds like it should, from Alpha female down to others, will impact Sarah's ability to control her shift throughout her pregnancy in a good way, ensuring a live birth."

I sat back, thinking. "So, if the female lycanthrope shifts while pregnant, it impacts the pup?"

Everyone around me nodded, their faces a variety of solemnness and sadness. These were wolves where miscarriage was common, all because of something that came naturally to them. Perhaps that is something I can research more.

Baron blew out air, standing and jostling Miranda out of his lap. She landed on her feet, turning to glower at her mate. He smiled and took her hand, walking to the door.

"Miranda and I have always wanted to explore the northern woods so we will take the rest of our Pack and head up there and establish a territory. Shane, you will take over this area in the south. Mercer wants to take Tessa and move to somewhere in between our Packs. He wouldn't tell me where, but with him between us, that should work fine. If needed, we can work together to deal with larger issues, such as if Edward shows his face again."

"Sounds good." Shane waved at the Alpha, before turning to Max. "Welcome to the Pack. It surprised me you wanted to come."

Max shrugged, standing. “It would be best for the baby. Besides that, I enjoy working with you.” He gave Shane a mischievous grin. “So, who will be your Beta? Or Betas?”

Shane groaned. “Splinter. But I think Shaz may have a chance. Boomer hates being responsible for others. That is why he works so well with Splinter. Boomer likes to work in the shadows.”

Max nodded. He turned to me.

“Now, about shifting...”

I shuddered. “I know nothing about that, Max.”

Shane lifted my hand and kissed it. “Have you ever felt like there is someone inside you? Something more than just you? Something that just wanted to get out?”

I thought back to when Edward had me chained down. “Yes, when Edward had me in his lab.”

Shane grimaced, before looking up at Max. “Do you think I should try to force her shift? Would it hurt her?”

I studied the doctor, his face pensive as he thought.

“I would say that if there isn’t a wolf there, it

shouldn't hurt her much. If there is, the first shift will be painful since she is so much older now than a typical first shift."

He turned back to me. "Holden?"

I nodded. "Let's try. I am not sure what you can do, but I would like to see if I can become a wolf." The excitement caused butterflies to flutter in my stomach.

Shane

I reached down my mate bond, searching for my mate's wolf. My wolf traveled with me, darting ahead and sniffing out corners in her mind. My wolf was eager to meet his wolf counterpart, her wolf self. I wasn't certain Holden even had a wolf. Nothing so far showed that she did.

My wolf leaped forward and rushed to a dark area deep in her core, startling me. I followed behind, my pace more hesitant.

There, in the darkness, a small reddish wolf cowered. My wolf whined, scratching at the darkness as if it was a solid wall, trying to get to his mate. I studied it. I wasn't sure what to do, but I didn't want to leave her wolf there, in the dark. Not if she could shift. I just didn't know what that darkness was or represented. Or where it came from.

I tried to reach in to grab the small wolf, but the gloom hid my hands. Nor could I feel her. I pulled back. I needed light. What was light?

Love.

I pushed my love and admiration of Holden towards the dark wall, trying to reach the wolf. I told her how much she meant to me – how much she had always meant to me since the first time I had met her. I showed her memories of when we had worked together, both in the distant past and now, letting her feel what I felt.

All the while, my wolf scratched and scrabbled, digging a hole in the darkness.

I wrapped her in love, talked to her about my wishes for our future, how we would live and grow together. About Lexi, Soren and Betta. About the new Pack, and our new life.

I felt the pups join with me in my mind, via the Pack bonds, and Maggie and Max, all sending their love to her. Lexi's light was so bright it outshone us all, but still the darkness caged the small wolf.

As my thoughts trailed off, uncertain what else to do, my wolf broke through enough that the small red wolf could push its head through. Both of us grabbed her and pulled.

Holden's mind threw me out as she shifted for the first time, her body changing into the reddish wolf. Her shift was swift, completing in minutes.

"Well, that was exciting." Max gave me an exhausted smile, as he knelt beside her, his hands traveling over the panting wolf. He would make sure we had done no damage to her by forcing her into a shift this first time.

I sighed, tired, my eyes running over my mate. She was beautiful. Smaller than she should have been, but that may have been because Holden's mind had somehow locked her in. I doubted she would ever had shifted if she hadn't had a mate and a Pack supporting her.

Her coat was a mix of thick red and brown fur, making her almost look like an older puppy puffball, or an older but less red version of Lexi. Her eyes were no longer just gray, but a green-gray color that stood out with her coat. She had points of black on her ears and her four paws were black. And there was a small, heart-shaped bit of white fur on her chest. To me, she looked almost like a fox, except bigger and leggier.

I smiled.

Holden, my mate, you are gorgeous. I sent my love down our bond.

Holden

I turned to look at Shane, my eyes glazed, but excited.

I am a wolf! Shane, I am a wolf! I turned my head this way and that, forcing Max to move to keep from bumping me.

You are. His grin got bigger.

All the smells! I didn't know there were so many smells. You smell great, like pine trees and… I stopped and gave a little sniff in his direction. *And spice!*

I turned and sniffed Max, yipping when he tapped me on the nose.

"Let me finish my examination, Holden."

Ha! He smells like grass and roses. I sneezed. *I think I am allergic to grass and flowers.* I grinned.

"You know I can hear you, Holden, right? You are not talking to Shane on the mate bond, but on the general Pack ones." Max's voice was absentminded, as he checked out my paws and then shone a light into my eyes. He sat back, looking up at Shane. "Perfect. Small, but perfect."

Shane chuckled. "And now we will never hear the end of this. The wolf biologist who is a wolf."

I got up and took a few steps before tripping and falling on my face.

Oomph! Walking with four legs is hard!

The men laughed.

A young girl's voice responded in my head. *Mama Holden! Let your wolf walk for you. Give her reign over your body because she knows what to do.*

Lexi? Is that you? I can talk to you even when I am a wolf?

You are Uncle Shane's mate now, part of the Pack.

You can talk to all of us - Betta, Soren and Maggie - at all times.

I stood up and danced around, my wolf keeping me on my feet as I moved about the room, ending up next to Shane, who was leaning forward, watching me, a huge grin on his face.

Thank you! Thank you! Thank you, Shane! But let's go for a run. I want to run! I want to...

I sat down and lifted my muzzle and howled, the sound a little weak at first but gaining in volume. A faint response came from the pups in the distance.

Shane couldn't resist. He shifted, his silver wolf rubbing up against me, his tail wagging.

You are huge! I looked at him, my eyes wide.

He laughed, giving me a playful nip on the ear. *That's what they all say*.

Huffing, I turned away. *You know what I meant*.

I watched as Max opened the cabin door before shifting himself. I approached the brown and gray wolf. *Hey, Max*!

Holden. I thought you wanted to run. The mirth in Max's tone came through on the bond.

I could hear Shane groan behind me as I moved out onto the porch. *Yes, let's run*.

I went to leap off the porch, but Shane was faster. He moved in front of me, stopping me from jumping and landing on my face again. He took the lead, nudging me into the direction he thought was best. We entered the woods and ran straight towards the compound, meeting the pups and Maggie about halfway there. Then our Pack ran deeper into the trees to show me what it was like to hunt and play in the woods as a wolf.

Hours later, Max peeled off to return to his mate and the rest of us headed back to the compound. The pups shifted and dressed. Shane shifted back, pulling on sweats before strolling into the kitchen to make dinner, while I waited impatiently, realizing that I had no clue how to shift back.

Lexi ran her hands through my fur. "Think of your human self, Mama. Imagine yourself as you always have been."

Shane turned as I shifted back, the shift going slower this time because I was building the image of myself in my mind. He reached down the mate bond and gave me a little push back into my human self, helping to speed up the shift.

Lexi got a blanket and threw it over me as I finished.

"That was hard!" I laid out flat on the deck, my lungs straining to get enough oxygen.

Betta, eating an apple, came and sat near me. "It will get easier, Mama." The little girl leaned against me, as if she needed the touch. Lexi leaned against my other side.

Soren, though, held himself apart from his sisters, watching us. Shane opened his mouth to speak, but I beat him to it.

"Soren." I sat up and my arms opened wide. The little boy jumped onto my lap, flinging his arms around my neck. "Don't become a serious Alpha too soon. I want to enjoy you as a little boy." I nuzzled his hair.

Chapter 22

Holden

The pups were sleeping when I walked out onto the back deck, looking up at the night sky. We had put them in the second bedroom, in the queen-size bed, for the night. Shane was on his computer in the living room, but I was feeling restless. I had come outside to breathe in the night air and observe the night.

Everything seemed more alive now. Now that I had the senses of a wolf. I could hear the smaller animals in the surrounding forest, burrowing in for the night or going out foraging for food. I could smell the trees and the flowers that were blooming nearby. And of the people living in my house.

This was different. This was new. But I was at peace.

A hand came around my waist, a blade held close to my neck. I breathed in, smelling nothing. Except someone held me immobile.

"Don't move, Holden. Not until I tell you to." The words slithered through the night air.

Edward.

How had he been able to mask his scent? How had he been able to hide his footsteps? Or had he been hiding here while we had been playing in the woods?

My panic flared and traveled down my Pack bond, alerting Shane and waking the pups, before I sent out an image of the knife at my neck.

"What are you doing here, Edward?" I tried to keep my voice calm, but a little wobble came through.

"Getting you back. Those wolves stole you from me. But you are mine. I saw you turn. You can become a wolf like they can. And yet, you are not a full lycanthrope. I will figure out your secret and I will sell it to the military. I will use it on myself. Perhaps then you will mate with me. Once I have killed that obnoxious male you have been hanging around with, you will have little option."

His voice was quiet, a hiss in my ear, as he pulled me back into the shadows on the deck.

I realized then that Edward knew nothing about wolves. Or at least none of the important things. Like how bonded mates would not have sex with anyone except their mate. Or how Packs could talk to each other without words, the communication effortless. He also didn't take into consideration that a Pack would protect all members, and that I was now part of a Pack.

"How do you expect to kill him? He is both a wolf and a military man. He has more skills as a human than you do." I wanted to keep him from looking for Shane, who had glided back towards the bedroom. I wanted to keep him from noticing the smaller black shadow that was Soren, creeping around the outside of the deck. The pup must have gone out the front door and then came back into the compound somehow, to circle around his prey like this.

Hunting wolves made no sound.

Warning ones growled, though.

A faint growl came from the house. Betta, in wolf form, and Lexi, as a little girl, moved into the living room.

"Damn it, those brats are up! I thought you put them to sleep."

"We did."

He swung me around, pushing me up against the railing, looking for the steps. Seeing them, he pulled me towards them. I tried to keep my balance, knowing my Pack was getting into place, that he wouldn't take me away from here. In fact, I wasn't sure he would survive tonight.

"Let's go. I don't need those brats anymore." Shadows crossed Edward's face. I could hear the ugliness in his voice as his greed for what the wolves had eluded him.

He had taken the first step down on the stairs when Soren flew out of the shadows and latched onto his upper thigh, very close to the man's genitals.

Edward screamed. He didn't let go of me, in fact he pulled me in tighter, while he grabbed the small wolf by the neck and tried to pull him off. The arm around my neck, which had been holding the knife, lowered. That was enough to change the balance of power.

“Let go, you fucking little rat!”

“Don’t call my brother a rat.” Lexi’s voice was firm. Betta, beside her, growled. The two girls had slipped out the doors onto the deck. Betta darted forward and bit Edward from behind, her teeth digging into his ass.

I wondered where Shane was, but perhaps we didn’t need him. The pups were taking their revenge on Edward, which they needed. In fact, there were a few things I wanted to do to him for kidnapping me. Particularly now that the knife rested on my collarbone instead of my neck.

This idiot had killed Thomas. As the thought rose in my mind, I growled and shoved an elbow back into Edward’s torso, my other hand coming up to hold the hand with the knife still. It slipped a little and cut me, but I didn’t feel it. I felt Betta pulling the man off balance from behind and Soren readjusting his mouth in front.

Someone grabbed the knife from his loose grip as I whirled around and jabbed my fist into Edward’s face, breaking his nose.

"You killed Thomas! There was no reason for you to kill Thomas, you asshat! He was your brother! He loved you!" Tears flowed down my face as I hit him again, his arms flying up to cover his face from the worst of my blows.

I didn't notice the pups drop off and move away, sitting to watch me, their eyes wide with amazement. I didn't notice that Shane was here, holding a gun pointed at Edward's back. I just released my anger, hitting the object of so much pain and mental anguish over and over, the sounds of my fists hitting his flesh loud in the night.

The man dropped to the deck, but I followed him down, straddling him, my fists flying.

Shane caught me around the middle, lifting me off the man, the gun still trained on him. Edward just laid on the deck, his hands over his head, his face bloody.

"Holden. Ease up, love. Those hands will hurt in the morning."

"He killed him, Shane. He killed him." I turned and buried my face in his shoulder.

Edward rolled over onto his front, his head in his

hands. Shane tracked his movements with the gun.

"I know, love. I know."

Shane

Car doors shut and footsteps rushed through the house.

"Out here, Baron." I didn't raise my voice, my eyes glued to the man who was now bleeding from bites to his leg and ass. His face was swelling from the beating Holden had given him.

Baron showed up and slowed. "Whoa. Who beat the crap out of him?"

I nodded at the two men with him. Splinter and Boomer each grabbed an arm and dragged Edward up between them. He swayed but somehow stayed standing, glowering at all of us as best he could with one eye swollen shut.

"Holden." I lowered the gun, putting the safety on and shoving it into my jeans at the small of my back, before wrapping both arms around Holden. "She needed to take out some of her anger on him. The pups got to have a taste."

Lexi giggled, while Soren turned his head away, huffing.

Baron just shook his head. "Don't get her mad, Shane. It looks like she hits hard." He jerked his head, and the two men dragged Edward off.

"She is mine!" He screamed at us. Splinter and Boomer stopped. I looked at him, my face void of emotion.

"She was never yours, Edward. She had been your brother's wife, but you killed him. She now is my mate. And you will never, ever get this close to her again. You have stolen and tortured my nieces and nephew. You have murdered my brother and his mate. You had taken and tortured my mate. You will not get your day in court. You will not get a judge and jury. Instead, we will try you based on Pack law. I am Alpha and I decree it. Take him."

Edward opened his mouth to scream out again, but Boomer turned into him and gave him a quick neck chop, catching him as the man went down, unconscious.

"One way to get him to shut the fuck up." Splinter chuckled. The two men then dragged him out of the compound.

Baron looked at me.

"Coming?"

I nodded, putting up a hand with five fingers up. Baron nodded and left, following the other two. Soon after, car doors shut, and the car started up.

"Come on, pups. Back to bed."

"Can we sleep with you?" Lexi moved towards me, patting Holden's leg. Holden's sobs had eased, but tears were still falling down her face. I rubbed her back, my nose dipping into her hair.

"I have to go out, Lexi, but you can sleep with Holden until I get back, okay? Protect her for me?"

All three of the pups nodded. Soren and Betta shifted back into kids and ran inside to get back into their pajamas, while Lexi followed me as I walked my mate to our bed. I took off her shoes and pulled off her jeans, tucking her under the covers. Lexi jumped up to cuddle on one side of her.

"Shane." Holden's voice tore my heart, but I needed to do this. I needed to bring her justice. This was my first act as Alpha of our Pack. She just didn't need to see this right now.

I leaned down, my lips touching her forehead.

Betta and Soren slipped into the room and crawled up the bed. Soren put himself on the other side of Holden, while Betta cuddled her sister. They would make sure no one could get to their mama.

Holden looked up at me, her eyes red. Her tears had stopped and her face looked calmer. "Thank you."

I leaned over and kissed her again, before walking out of the bedroom.

Holden

Waking up, I realized that I was alone in the bed. I didn't remember Shane coming back. I knew, though, that the pups had been here, in my bed, most of the night.

I could hear sounds in the kitchen, so I got up,

taking care of my morning routine, before shuffling out of the bedroom. So much had happened in so little time.

Shane was there, making breakfast.

"Where are the pups?" I drifted over to the island, sitting on the stool. My hands hurt. My body hurt. And my head ached from all my crying.

Shane gave me a glass of water and two pain reliever pills. He then pushed a mug of coffee with milk and sugar next to them on the counter.

"Max came and took them. Take the pills and then I will wrap your hands." He stood there, waiting for me to do as he asked.

I picked up the pills and held them. "What happened to Edward?"

Shane exhaled. "Take the pills, Holden. Please."

Glowering at him, I popped them into my mouth and then took a sip of water. "There. Now tell me."

Shane turned back to the stove and scooped out scrambled eggs onto a plate, which already held a few strips of bacon. He placed it near my hand and gave me a fork, before moving around to sit next to me.

“Pack law.” He turned to me and watched my face. “No one will find him. No one will know. Mercer even came to take part because Edward had held him for almost a year. Tortured him for almost a year. Edward had made him shift back and forth at the man’s whim, sometimes up to ten times a day.” Shane’s voice was rough with anger.

I just looked at him. “So, he’s dead.” There was no emotion in my voice.

He nodded twice.

“Good. It was more than he deserved.” I turned around and picked up the mug, sipping at my coffee.

Shane stared at me. “You don’t mind we killed him?”

I reached over and grabbed my phone. Accessing my pictures, I pulled up one and put the phone down between us. It was the picture that Edward had sent me of Thomas pleading with him for help.

“The man that did that to another human being - no, not just another human being, but his brother - shouldn’t get human justice of a few years of prison. Jail is too good for him after what he had done. He deserves to die. We should treat him like the vermin he was."

He looked at me. I am sure he was wondering how much this would change me. Or if I would have regrets later. Heck, I was wondering how much I had already changed to accept this all so easy.

I sighed, putting down my fork, still staring at my plate. "Did Mercer feel vindicated?"

"Yes."

Turning just my head, I met his eyes. "Good. Then I am fine with his punishment." I sat up and swung myself around. "Thank you for protecting me, Shane. Thank you for being here with me and for coming back for me."

My hands cupped his face, my fingers stroking his skin.

"I know little about being a lycanthrope, but I know some about wolves. I know wolves would be fine with this. I know that this is one area where they are kinder than humans are, given it was over with quickly. Edward living forever in jail would have been scary. Human courts would have released him, allowing him to commit more crimes. He was not sane. But he could act sane when he wanted to."

I got up and moved between his legs, putting my arms around his neck. "Now, I want you to either take me to my pups or make love to me. Your choice, Alpha." My smile was soft, but the love I had for this man that was radiating down the bond must have convinced him which option I wanted him to choose.

No more talk about Edward. Or Thomas. Or labs.

Just about us and our future.

Shane pulled me in and kissed me, his mouth hungry as it moved over mine. Picking me up, I wrapped my legs around his waist as he moved towards our bedroom.

"What? Not the pups?" I teased him.

"Pups later. It is just about us. I love you, Holden Black."

I laughed, feeling happy for the first time in a long time. "And I love you, Shane Loren! Forever and always!"

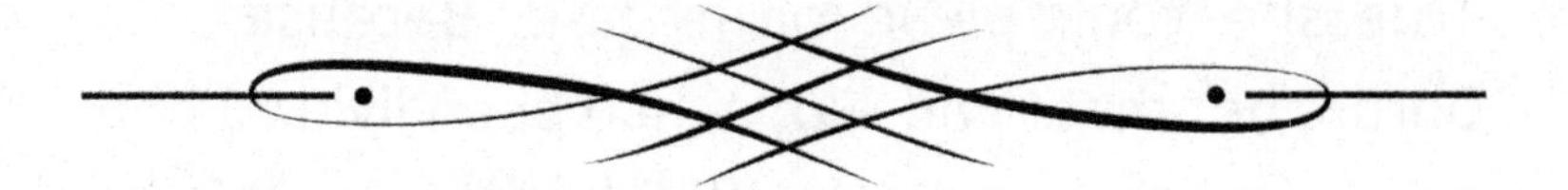

You can sign up for my newsletter and get ***The Prophecy***, the FREE prequel that explains more about why Holden is different from other lycanthropes here.

The next book in the series is Berserker, which goes into Tessa and Mercer's story, as well as why Tessa is they way she is.

Chapter 1

Loneliness has a scent, and I reeked of it.

I sniffed, turning to stare out the window.

My sister had left me here. Here alone. While she went back to her Pack.

True, she would plead for my case. Because Baron, her mate and Alpha, had been livid to find out I had been working with Edward.

I sneered. Edward Black had caused all of this. He had approached me, talking about how he knew lycanthropes existed and how he needed help to get access to some. He had told me how he planned to make us better, that he could get me any mate I wanted.

And I had wanted Shane Loren.

I also needed help. Help from someone who could keep my secrets.

There was more than just me and my wolf inside my body. I wasn't sure what else there was. But that other part of me scared me. I had wanted to talk to Edward about it, but I hadn't been sure I could trust him.

Well, that had been a bust. He was not worth my reputation, which I lost anyway. The Pack would kill me for what I had done.

I froze.

That could literally be true. I wasn't sure what the punishment was for aiding someone like Edward, but I suspected it just might be death.

I shook my head, standing up and walking over to a window to stare out into the trees. I crossed my arms over my chest and rubbed one hand on my upper arm.

My sister wouldn't allow Baron to kill me, would she? She was the Alpha female. She could influence my punishment. Mira loved me.

Oh, please, let her have enough influence. I wasn't ready to die yet.

What if I was like Mami? What if I changed into a beast? Would Miranda be able to get me to change back? She knew how Papi did it with Mami. But then she would be my anchor.

I snorted. It would be a disaster if Mira was my anchor!

I blew on the window, my breath making a fog there. I ran a finger through the condensation, a slight squeak disturbing the quiet.

Winter was coming. And I didn't want to spend it here in this cabin, all by myself.

I doubted the Alpha would forgive what I did. I didn't want to become the low wolf – lower than even Maggie. I would die if they ranked me at the bottom of the Pack. If they made me fight to even stay in the Pack. Then again, perhaps that was better than dying or staying out here alone.

No. I would leave before they humiliated me like that!

I listened on the Pack bonds. Nothing. No whispers of people talking, no feelings leaking through. Baron must have cut me off from the Pack.

I still had my bond with Miranda, but even that felt muffled. My wolf could hear nothing more than whispers.

That other part of me rose, allowing me to somehow hear her thoughts, working around the block that was put on our bond. The whispers got louder, the words clearer. I didn't care how I could hear her, though. I had to know what was going on.

"Our parents weren't part of a Pack, Baron. They were...... a pair of lone wolves that had gotten together to have pups. Tessa and me. We all kept to ourselves and they spoiled us rotten. When I

had met and mated with you, my parents had been so angry with me. They had tried to stop all of my communication with my sister, but we somehow got notes to one another. When Tessa had shown up, telling me that our parents had died, I knew I had to take care of her. I had left her with them, and then she had no one else to turn to."

Miranda was talking with someone, perhaps Baron, her mate. She was telling them about our family. She was begging for me. Good.

But then I felt a numbness come over her mind. What was going on? What were they saying to her?

"I am sorry that she caused so much disruption to the Pack."

Darn! It didn't sound like anyone would let me off. I don't think anyone knew I had lied to Miranda about our parents being dead. I could go home.

I grimaced, chewing on my lip.

My fear was that if she had known they were still alive, she wouldn't have taken me in. That she would have made me return to them.

I didn't want to go back. I just might not have a choice. Mami had locked us up all our lives, not letting us interact with others. All because of her own secret!

I turned, leaning against the window. What if Mira had found out I lied?

Mira, my sweet older sister, whom everyone loved.

I couldn't understand why that Alpha had chosen her over me. I was prettier than my sister. More ambitious. Tougher.

I would have been a better Alpha female than her. She was just too....nice.

I couldn't understand why none of the males — single or mated — wanted me.

Perhaps somehow, they could feel that I was different inside, even though I wasn't sure what that difference was.

I sighed. Others shied away from me for no reason. I never understood it, but it must have been something about me. Something I could feel but not quite identify.

I am sure that was what drove Shane away. Look

at whom he had ended up with — that human. Weak.

Well, if Edward was correct, she was a hybrid of some sort. Still weak. Unable to change and fight.

Not a fierce wolf, like I was.

I stood up, moving towards the bedroom. I had to go. Miranda would be angry with me if she found out our parents lived. While she had hidden me here, she would eventually tell them where I was. And they would come for me.

Perhaps it was time to go home.

My parents will allow me to stay until I could figure things out. Where to go. What to do.

I hoped.

They were far enough away from the Pack that they wouldn't have heard about the Hybrid or Edward. Or my part in that situation either. With Miranda still thinking they are dead — hopefully — the Pack wouldn't come for me there.

I stood in the bedroom. What should I take with me?

I looked around. There was little here I wanted.

Some clothes, some food, some money.

All of my current life would fit in a backpack. I ran into the bathroom, stopping to look at myself in the mirror.

Honey blond hair fell down my back, bracketing my face. Light brown eyes stared back at me. I studied that face for a moment.

I had classical features, different from Miranda, who had darker hair and eyes. She looked more like our father, while I was a carbon copy of my mother.

I huffed, pulling up my hair into a high pony tail and then braiding the loose strands so it fell to my shoulders, but stayed out of my face. I grabbed my things out of there and then strode back into the bedroom. Dumping everything on the bed, I went to the closet and pulled out my backpack, quickly stuffing my clothes inside it.

My wolf was silent, but something made me uneasy. I listened to those instincts.

I needed to leave. Now.

I finished packing my things before moving into the kitchen.

Food. I needed to take some food. I could hunt, but I didn't want to leave my backpack anywhere while I did so. Not if I didn't have to.

I felt the pressure growing to leave, that it was more important than bringing food with me.

I grunted before grabbing a handful of chocolate bars and stuffing them in my backpack. As much as eating meat was satisfying for my wolf, my human side needed chocolate.

I moved to the front door, looking out at the area in front of it.

There wasn't much of a clearing there, so someone could hide within the trees. They could ambush me when I left.

But...

I didn't think anyone had come here yet. Miranda wouldn't give me up that fast. At least, I hoped she wouldn't.

I stepped out on the porch and sniffed, using my nose to discover anything unusual. It wasn't as good as my nose as a wolf, but it was better than a typical human one.

Nothing.

Yet something was pushing me to go east. It didn't want me to take the path to the west. That was where the Pack was. It was directing me away from the Pack. I agreed.

Readjusting my backpack on my shoulders, I stepped down off the porch and headed out, noting that I had at least four hours before dark.

I felt a little sorry I hadn't left a note for my sister, but if she could give me up, it was best she didn't know where I was. I repositioned the bag on my shoulders once more and entered the woods.

I didn't see the gleaming yellow eyes watching me within the trees. Nor did I see the wolf they belonged to slink after me, his steps silent. He moved almost like he was a shadow passing through the trees.

Or like he was hunting...

Me.

Author's Notes

It has taken me some time to get from my last series to this one. Partly because of just learning the trade of Indie publishing. Partly because of my health. And partly because of fear. I wanted to be the best that I could be now.

But writing is like taking that first step. And then the second. Those steps are scary. Necessary, but scary. There is so much to learn on this journey, but foremost is to put words on paper. Without the stories, the rest mean little.

Hybrid is the first of the Rare Wolf Series.

If you want to get the Prequel that explains why Holden is different from other lycanthropes, you can sign up for my newsletter to get The Prophecy.

You can find me at the following places:

https://www.facebook.com/kjcarrauthor

http://kjcarr-author.com

Other Books By K J Carr

Immortal Transformation Series

Immortal Decisions

Immortal Transition

Immortal Vengeance

Immortal Transformation Universe

Achilah

Rare Wolf

Hybrid
Berserker
Omega
Alemos
Warrior
Protector

Rare Wolf Novellas

Merry Soul-fill Christmas

Gatekeeper
Miranda

Printed in Great Britain
by Amazon